THROUGH THE BACKDOOR

SON OF IMMIGRANT PARENTS OVERCOMES MANY OBSTACLES TO BECOME A PHYSICIAN

Peter C. Gazes, M.D.

PREFACE

In this story of my life, I will describe the obstacles I overcame to become a doctor. Humor was a part of all my lectures because I found it relaxed both my audience and me. It was not intended to distract from the serious aspects of my medical narrative. A touch of laughter is needed in every physician's stressful life. The incidents described are recorded as I remember them. I have strived to be as accurate as possible. Some of the people mentioned are deceased. I hope my story will encourage young people to have the determination, persistence, and motivation to achieve all they desire in life. In wonderful America I have—*through the back door.*

DEDICATION

To my wife, Athena and my three daughters, Hope, Catherine, and Joanne, who have patiently supported and inspired me.

ACKNOWLEDGEMENTS

I am eternally grateful to my family, Athena, Hope, Catherine, and Joanne who have contributed to this book through their support and computer expertise. I owe a special thanks to my good friend, Richard Shreadly, former editor of the combined News and Courier and Evening Post of Charleston, South Carolina, who reviewed this book and gave many excellent suggestions. I wish to express special gratitude to Linda Paddock, who typed the manuscript in a computer format and also onto a disk and to my patients and medical personnel who had confidence in me. The staff of CreateSpace were very helpful, especially Zachary Coddington, senior publishing consultant.

DISCLAIMER

The author has presented factual information, but this book is not intended to provide medical advice. The incidents described were recorded as remembered and documented. I have strived to be as accurate as possible. Some of the people mentioned are deceased. The many stories were my originals and others passed down by my friends and patients.

THROUGH THE BACK DOOR
The Making of a Doctor

Peter C. Gazes, M.D., F.A.C.C., M.A.C.P.
Professor of Medicine
Distinguished Clinical University Professor of Cardiology
Medical University of South Carolina
College of Medicine
Charleston, South Carolina

"Nothing in the world can take the place of persistence. Talent will not; nothing is more common than unsuccessful men with talent. Genius will not; unrewarded genius is almost a proverb. Education will not: the world is full of educated derelicts. Persistence and determination alone are omnipotent."

Calvin Coolidge

TABLE OF CONTENTS

Medicine at the Crossroads

CHAPTER I
EARLY YEARS
Persistence, Motivation, Determination, and Laughter

I have always considered that persistence, determination, and motivation will determine one's future, regardless of gender, race, religion, or wealth. This is the story of my life. I had to overcome many obstacles, including bigotry and prejudice, to become a physician. My success did not come easily but rather *through the back door.*

My father came to America from Greece in 1905 to find a better life. His ship brought him to New York, and a Greek church group sent him by train to Sumter, South Carolina. Greeks are very proud of where they came from in Greece. Since he came from the island of Cephalonia, he was sent to Sumter, where another Greek from Cephalonia operated a fruit stand. While working there, he became enchanted with nearby St. Matthews, a small town divided by railroad tracks. After several years, he saved enough to purchase a general merchandise store there. He eventually bought several buildings by the tracks. He often visited Charleston and occasionally attended the Greek Church there. By chance the priest had known his parents.

A young man once went to a Greek priest and asked if he would give a memorial service on behalf of his dog. The priest said, "I don't have time, but I will call the Episcopal priest up the road. I am sure he would do it." So the fellow said, "When you call him, tell him that there is a $10,000 donation." The priest turned and said, "Why didn't you tell me the dog is Greek Orthodox?"

After a time, my father decided to revisit his homeland. His parents were determined that he should marry before he returned to America, and they selected the woman who would become his wife (and my mother), as was the custom then. She was an attractive, gracious, kind person; soft spoken and well-educated, my mother was fluent in several languages. She often took food and clothing to the poor. During the years my parents lived in St. Matthews, she bore five children—two girls and three boys. I was the youngest.

My mother insisted that we move to Charleston, so that her children could get a better education. My father sold his property, and we moved. He bought Greek bonds with his money, intending that after a few years we would go back to Greece. The bonds became worthless, and he never returned to his native land. He went back every year to visit St. Matthews. He died when he was ninety-five.

I was six-months-old when we moved to Charleston, and now my story begins.

My father was small in stature but very muscular. He stood straight and walked briskly. Since he was over forty-years-old when he got married, I only knew him with a moustache, thinning, gray hair, and small-rimmed eyeglasses. He worked tirelessly. However, he always took at least a one-hour midday nap. He was devoted to his family but would never show his emotions. We all realized he was very strict and tried not to upset him. Honesty was his best trait. Often deliverymen would bring an extra sack of rice that they had stolen from their employer and offered this to my father at a lower price. My father would immediately report them. His education was limited, but he had a fantastic memory. The only recreation he enjoyed was walking on the beach at 5:00 A.M. since his store opened at 7:00 A.M.

Our first home was on the north side of Charleston over my father's grocery store. One day, when I was about four-years-old, I was playing Tarzan with my brother Jimmy. He placed a rope over the upstairs porch balcony and pulled me up from the ground. The rope broke, and I fell hard on the right side of my chest. Because my father was so strict, I promised Jimmy that I would not tell what happened even though I was in severe pain. Several days later, the pain became worse, and I began running a high fever. My mother took me to a doctor. I had a broken rib and infection had set in. There were no antibiotics then, and the infection had to be drained daily through a tube in my chest. I was in the hospital for several weeks and still have a scar on the right side of my chest.

Many sailors from ships visiting Charleston came to our grocery store, and one time they gave my father a parrot. The parrot was over fifty-years-old, and we taught him to speak English and Greek. I have a lot of parrot jokes, and here is one of them:

A man told his wife to buy a parrot because his boss was coming to dinner, and his boss liked parrots. She went to a shop, and the owner said that the only parrot available had belonged to a prostitute, but she bought it anyway. While in the car, the parrot said, "New owner, new car." At home the parrot said, "New owner, new car, new home." A daughter and her girlfriend had just returned from college, and the parrot said, "New owner, new car, new home, and new girls". At this moment the husband came in with his boss, and the parrot said, "New owner, new car, new home, new girls but the same old clients."

We next moved to an area west of town called Gadsden Green and into an apartment above another grocery store. We children liked this part of town for we could play baseball, at low tide, in a field near our home. It was near the Ashley River Bridge. The Charleston peninsula has two rivers—the Cooper on the east and the Ashley on the west. The locals say they meet to form the Atlantic Ocean.

The grocery store served the surrounding neighborhood for at that time there were no supermarkets. My father operated many grocery stores in his lifetime, but this one was unique and interesting. The interior of the store had the charm of an old country store. An old potbelly stove stood in the center of the store to provide heat. It is named for its bulging center, and it burns wood or coal. Sacks of rice, flour, grits, and various nuts lined one side of the wall. Grits are a corn-based food common in the southern states. The corn for grits is ground by a millstone, and the results pass through screens with the finer part being corn and the coarse being grits. Grits are served with butter and salt but seldom with sugar. They are also served with shrimp, cheese, or eggs.

The shelves around the store displayed canned goods. There were several bins that were loaded with colorful displays of fruits and vegetables. Each morning one could see the vendors crossing the Ashley River Bridge on their horse-drawn wagons that were filled with vegetables, namely collards and turnip greens that came from the farms to be sold to the merchants. In addition, chewing tobacco, cigars, cigarettes, snuff, and pipe tobacco were common items for sale. It was not unusual to see farmers sitting in chairs in the back of the store smoking tobacco in their corncob pipes before buying groceries. They also enjoyed eating sweet potatoes that were cooked on the potbelly stove.

The main meats for sale were boloney, ham, ham hock, fatback (also called butts meat), sardines, and pickled pig's feet. Ham hock is the joint between the foot and leg of a hog. Fatback is the large layer of fat along the back of the pig. It is a traditional part of southern cooking. Fatback and ham hock are often used to flavor stewed vegetables and black-eyed peas. The poor often fried fatback and ate it with grits or rice. The meats were stored in iceboxes because mechanical refrigeration was not available. The iceboxes were made of wood and often resembled a piece of furniture. They had hollow walls that were lined with tin or zinc and packed with insulating material such as cork, sawdust, straw, or seaweed. A large block of ice was held in a tray or compartment at the top of the box. Cold air circulated down and around the storage compartment in the lower section. Some iceboxes had spigots for draining ice water, and others had only a drip pan under the box that had to be emptied daily. Ice companies delivered ice to the various stores.

A father listened to his son's prayer. "God bless father, mother, grandmother, and good- bye dog." The next day the dog was found dead. The boy prayed that night. "God bless father and mother, and good-bye grandmother." The next morning the grandmother was found dead. Again, the father heard his son's prayer, "God bless mother, and good-bye father." The father did not sleep well, and the next morning he carefully drove to work. On returning home he told his wife he had a rough day. His wife answered, "I had a worse day. Our delivery iceman dropped dead."

Our grocery store served as a community center. Many came for Coca-Cola, different sodas, snacks, and lots of conversation. Children came for frozen bananas coated with chocolate, Popsicles, snowballs, and Dixie cup ice cream. The snowballs were finely shaven ice, covered with a choice of flavored syrup. The Dixie cup had ice cream of various flavors, and the back of the top cover had pictures of animals. Often these pictures were changed for a movie star or a baseball player.

Just outside of our grocery store, watermelons were stacked against the wall. My father had me sell them. Since it was boring work, I placed a large barrel that was used for shipping fruits next to the watermelons. The barrel was turned upside down and Taso, a friend, got inside. He was a gifted drummer and used two sticks to beat against the inside of the barrel. At the same time, I got on top of the barrel and pretended that I was tap dancing. People would buy watermelons and place money at my feet.

We lived in the apartment above the store, and while it had many rooms, there was only one bathroom that had to be reached from an open porch. The kitchen was very small and cooking was done with gas. Ice was placed daily in the icebox that stored many items. My two brothers and I slept in the attic. There was no central heat, and we moved small kerosene heaters from room to room as necessary.

During the summer it was extremely hot, and air-conditioning was not available. At 11:00 P.M., most of the Greek families would close their stores and go to White Point Gardens and the Battery to relax and enjoy the cool breezes off the Ashley and Cooper Rivers. The name White Point was used for the lower peninsula of the city, and the fortification was the Battery. The Battery is protected from the rivers by a seawall. Next to the seawall was a lower walk that rises and becomes the high Battery, where many people often strolled in the late afternoon. Beyond the seawall, Fort Sumter can be seen in the distance. The Civil War began on April 12, 1861, when the Confederates began firing on the Union-held Fort Sumter. On display in the park are cannon from the war as well as cannon balls cemented in piles. Also in the park there was a large bandstand where there was a concert each Sunday. On the other side of the park and along the waterfront of the Battery there were many majestic mansions. Each home has a marker indicating its significance and the date of construction. On the front and back of the houses there were washers or bolts on the outside walls. These secured iron rods. The iron rods went from one end of the house to the other to reinforce and give protection to the house. They were installed after the severe earthquake in Charleston in 1886. Often today washers are added to new construction to emulate the old look for decorative purposes.

Each family brought food to share when they went to the battery. One fat, jolly man in the group brought a bedpan filled with spaghetti and meatballs. This was one of his many antics to amuse his friends. He would eat, and then sit on the bedpan and offer some of the spaghetti and meatballs to the others. To many this was disgusting, but to him it was funny.

Many adults would fish from the Battery. On one occasion I brought a long cord and tied a bent nail on the end of it. From the food that we brought with us, I took a piece of shrimp and attached it to the nail. I used a small brick as a sinker. I threw the line into the river, and low and behold I caught a spot tail bass. I was so excited. I ran with the fish to my mother. No one could believe that with the homemade equipment, I could catch such a fish.

After eating, the children climbed on the cannon and also played on the bandstand pretending they were actors and entertained the adults in this fashion.

Eventually, after all the activities at the park, the children fell asleep on the green grass until 2:00 A.M. when all families departed.

Sunday was a special day for our family. We had to bathe in a large washtub because there was no running warm water. Greek families in Charleston were close, and every Sunday after church, we would gather at different homes.

We could not afford a newspaper, and I liked to see the Sunday funny pages, so I convinced my parents to visit some friends who subscribed to the paper. They lived on a farm that had a large barn that was painted red. The loft was used to store hay and grains, and there were stalls on the lower floor for large animals. In the corner of the barn there was a pile of hay. On one occasion, I went into the barn to pee and to hide from my older brother Jimmy and his friend. On entering the barn there was a strong odor of hay and straw. I covered myself with straw so they could not find me. They came in and unfortunately they peed on my pile of straw not realizing I was hiding under it. I began to cry and took off all my clothes. It was late, and my mother wondered where I was. Jimmy finally told her what happened. She had to bring clean clothing before I would come out.

Another time when we visited a Greek family, all the adults sat in a circle in the living room, and the children played in the center. My brother Jimmy was lifting kids above his head, and I decided I would lift one too. As I strained to do it, I farted and dropped him. I thought quickly and cried, "Bad boy." The boy's mother spanked him. When he grew up, he became a Greek Orthodox priest and had a parish in Savannah, Georgia. He invited me to give a talk during one of his retreats. I spoke about diet and the four Lenten periods (Easter, lent of Peter and Paul, Holy Mother Mary, and Christmas). I didn't mention the farting incident. Neither did he.

It was a great treat to see a movie. I had to do many odd jobs to get enough money to buy a ticket. In between the main movie, prizes were often given to those who had the winning number on their ticket stub. One time, I won a large watermelon. I was so happy as I ran up onto the stage to accept my prize. Coming back, I slipped, and the watermelon smashed on the floor. I cried.

Christmas is one of my favorite holidays. Some Christmas days, I'd go outside and see children dressed in cowboy suits, riding bicycles, and skating. My father's grocery store provided just enough to keep up with home expenses. He could not afford gifts. This did not disturb me because I understood why there were no gifts. One time, I did get a pair of skates from Mr. Garbis, a family friend. The skates had brackets that you attached to the front and back of your shoes with screws. Since my shoes were very worn, the skates would not stay on, and I had to tie them on with a cord. Sometimes the soles of my shoes came off when I was skating, making me fall. One Christmas I made a wagon out of parts from a junkyard. I got four wheels and connected them, front and back with a wooden bar. Since many grocery stocks came in small barrels, I used one to make the body of the wagon. This gave it the shape of a race car. I had fun with that with my friends—another *through the back door* moment.

My father was a taskmaster and insisted that his children work in the grocery store. My brother Pat enjoyed it, but my brother Jimmy and I often stepped out to one of the playgrounds. We knew if found out, we would get a beating, but it was worth it. To this day, I support neighborhood playgrounds. I was a baseball pitcher and not having a regular ball to practice with, I made one by wrapping string around a small rubber core. I found pieces of old leather and sewed them on the ball. This was my practice baseball. A week came when we had a tournament, and I pitched five consecutive games. The night before the final game for the championship my brother massaged my sore arm. The next day I could hardly move it. My first pitch was hit for a homerun, and we lost in a rout

We sometimes played a game called "half rubber" with a small rubber ball cut in half. We played between two buildings and used a broomstick for a bat. A single, double, triple, or home run depended on how far you hit the half ball. This taught us to be good hitters. Talking of baseball…

An Italian brought his mother to visit him in America. One Sunday, he said, "Mom, I'm going to take you to a baseball game. Many Italians play this game." At the ballpark he said she should encourage the players by clapping and yelling every time they got a hit. The first batter for the Yankees was Phil Rizzuto. The son tapped his mother on the shoulder and said, "He's one of us." Phil Rizzuto got a single, and the mother jumped up and yelled, "Run, Phil, run." The son said, "That's the way, Mom." The next batter was Yogi Berra, and the son said he was also Italian. Yogi got a single and the mother jumped up again and yelled, "Run, Yogi, run." The son said the next batter was the best of them all, Joe DiMaggio, and he is Italian, too. There was a man on first and second, and they decided to walk Joe. The mother jumped up and said, "Run, Joe, run." The son said, "No, Mom. Joe has four balls." She yelled, "Walk proud, Joe, walk proud."

Our father insisted we attend Greek school in the afternoon after elementary school. At night, we worked at the grocery store. A wonderful Greek teacher one day caught me reading my school lessons in class because I did not have time to study at home. He realized the importance of education and told me to continue what I was doing and not worry because I'd get a passing grade in Greek. Another through-the-back-door experience.

Because of whooping cough, I missed the third year of elementary school and had to study at home. I did very well on my examination and was given the chance to take the fourth-year exam as well. I passed that, too, and they allowed me to skip fourth grade. I graduated with first honors from elementary school, and my reward was a fountain pen. It was given by a local pharmacist who was on the school board.

A young man had a date, and before going to the girl's home, he stopped at a drugstore to buy some condoms. The pharmacist realized that he had never used these before and explained how it was done. That night when he went to pick up his date, her family insisted that he stay for dinner. He was asked to give the blessing. With his head down low, he prayed slowly for several minutes. His girlfriend looked at him and said, "I didn't know you were so religious." He looked at her and said, "I didn't know your father was a pharmacist."

My next level of education was at the High School of Charleston, which was then segregated by race and gender. Since I could not afford a bicycle, I made one from parts gathered at a junkyard. However, it was not reliable, and I only would ride it in our neighborhood. Walking to school took at least thirty minutes. We didn't fear walking anywhere then. There was very little crime. Senator Fritz Hollings is a close friend. At times his uncle, a successful attorney, gave us a ride to school in his car.

A young man asked if he could drive his father's new car. The father said there were three stipulations: one, he had to raise his grades from Cs to Bs; two, he had to read the Bible every night; and three, he had to cut his long hair. After three months, the boy went to the father and stated, "I have done what you told me." The father said, "Yes, I noticed you have increased your grades from Cs to Bs and that you read the Bible every night, but you did not cut your long hair." The boy answered "I noticed while reading the Bible that Christ and the disciples had long hair." The father answered, "But did you notice that they walked wherever they wanted to go?"

I inherited clothes from my older brothers. One pair of pants had been worn so much that the seat was shiny. Fellow students would have me bend over and use it as a mirror to comb their hair—at least that's what they said. In high school, I played football starting as quarterback on the B team. One game I remember very well was with the Leopold Pals from Savannah, Georgia. Leopold was a Greek who had an ice cream company and sponsored the team. It so happened their backfield was made up of Greeks, and they called their plays in Greek. I knew every play they called, and we defeated them.

We moved again to another grocery store with living quarters above. It was on King Street in Charleston. It was heated by a kerosene stove that we moved from room to room as needed. On cold mornings, we had to run across the porch to get to the bathroom that we all shared.

I inherited a summer job selling soft drinks to other stores from my brother Jimmy. This was a learning experience. Soft drinks came in bottles and were carried in wooden crates. When I delivered drinks, I had to pick up an equal number of empty bottles, otherwise I was charged for them. Some store operators always had two to three missing bottles, and when they made up a full crate from missing bottles, they asked for a refund. They did not realize that I kept an account of missing bottles. Pepsi-Cola had just come on the market, and at night we had to stick the paper labels on the bottles by hand. At first, Pepsi was not very popular but eventually became a big seller. In fact, my boss stopped selling other soft drinks. The older employees often played tricks on me. One day they sent me to deliver a crate of Pepsi-Cola to a place that I did not know on the west side of town. When I arrived at the address, I saw many women wearing skimpy clothing. Some were wearing only bras and panties. Others were in bathrobes partially opened. They began to open my shirt and rub my chest, kissing my neck and ear. I could feel hands reaching into my trousers. I did not know it was a whorehouse. When I went to collect, the madam said "Why don't you take it out on trade as the others do?" It was very tempting because I was aroused. However, I took the payment and ran out through the back door.

A man told his wife-to-be that he was an avid golfer and that on Saturday he would not cut the grass or do any other home chores. She said she had a confession too: "I am a hooker." He said, "That's no problem; just turn your left hand a bit more underneath the club."

Our grocery store on King Street was famous for a popcorn machine at the entrance and our Greek- and English-speaking parrot that sat on an open bar with two cups of food on either side. I taught the parrot to say "Nice kids, penny please" to schoolkids passing by. Once they put a penny in the cup, if they tried to retrieve it, he would bite at them. At the end of the day, I usually had enough pennies to buy my favorite sweet roll at a nearby bakery shop.

Three ministers and their wives were killed in an auto accident and went to heaven. St. Peter told the first one, "You were a good minister but loved money so much you married a girl named Penny." He looked at the second one and said, "You were a good minister but you liked wine so much you married a girl named Sherry." The third minister grabbed his wife by the hand and said, "Fanny, we better get out of here."

One Sunday, my family decided to go on a short trip and left me to run the grocery store. It was a cold day, and I saw two eyes and a pair of lips pressed against the frosted front store window. It was a black boy, and I asked him to come in. I was cooking sweet potatoes on our wooden potbelly stove that heated the store. He ate one and then swept the floor for me. Subsequently, he worked for us and grew to be a very dedicated employee. Since he had flat feet, we named him Floogie. "Flat Foot Floogie" is an old jazz song and dance.

I graduated with first honors from the High School of Charleston and was given the choice of giving the valedictory or salutatory address at commencement. Our principal insisted that I give the latter since I had four years of Latin and the salutatory was given in Latin. Many colleges recognized only the valedictorian as the first honor. For this reason, the Citadel, the Military College of South Carolina, did not accept me. I was fortunate to get a scholarship at the College of Charleston. This was better for me since I do not think I would have adapted well to a military school. At that time, the College of Charleston had only 500 students and classes were very small. Many of students at the college went on to medical school and this was my desire. I also had taken the entrance examination for admission to the U.S. Naval Academy. Since I had no money, I did this with the hope of becoming a navy medical officer. I reviewed questions on the exam with my high school teachers, and I knew that I did well. However, this was a political appointment, and our congressman selected a person who did not even take the exam.

We did not have much during my early years, but we enjoyed what we had. I had some obstacles to overcome, and I did so *through the back door*.

CHAPTER 2
CHARLESTON COLLEGE AND MEDICAL SCHOOL
Energetic and Hard Working

Since I did not have any money or connections, I majored in mathematics with the intention to become a teacher until I found a way to enter medical school. Being of Greek heritage, even though I was born in America, I knew that Greeks were not well accepted in Charleston. Many clubs, even to this day, will not accept Greeks who attend the Orthodox Christian Church. I was blackballed on several occasions even though my sponsors were outstanding citizens. Some members of these clubs think Greeks are not Christian. The churches were all one until the schism of 1054, when the Orthodox went east and the Catholics went west. The Orthodox branch is made up of not only Greeks but Russians and others. In fact, the New Testament was originally written in Greek. The Orthodox liturgy today is the same as it was before the schism, but mainly in the language of the country. Immigrants from Greece established churches not only for their religion but also for friendship. Because of this, many non-Greeks begin their conversation with Greeks by mentioning the Greek Festival. Greeks are known more for their cooking than their religion. Being misinformed is not unusual and is depicted in this story:

An alcoholic went into a bar and asked for a drink. The bartender said, "You already have had too much." He said, "If I show you an act will you give me a drink?" The bartender said, "Yes." The alcoholic pulled a small piano from one pocket and a mouse dressed in tails from the other pocket. The mouse began to

play, and everyone was amazed. After a while the bartender said, "No more drinks."
The alcoholic said, "If I add on to this act, will you give me another drink?" He said,
"Yes," and the alcoholic pulled a canary from his pocket. The mouse played the
piano, and the canary sang to everyone's amazement. The bartender said, "Will you
sell the act?" He said, "Yes, for $500." The bartender said wait here and I will get
the money from the bank across the street. Another person at the bar overheard
the conversation and told the alcoholic, "You are crazy to sell that act for only $500.
In Hollywood you could get millions." The alcoholic answered, "This is a hoax. That
canary can't sing. The mouse is a ventriloquist."

While in college, I worked in my father's grocery story and at night at
Mike's, a sandwich shop across from the medical school. Mike was short in
stature and had a prominent belly. He had fluffy black hair with a speck of
gray. Usually he wore short- sleeved shirts of different colors and baggy pants.
He was a kind and considerate person. Often he would leave me in charge of
the shop, so that he could help freshman medical students find living quarters.
Many of the students' parents had completed their studies at the medical
school. World War II was in progress. He kept up with the daily events, which
many physicians came in to hear from him. Working at Mike's was a wonderful and interesting experience. Mike's had slot machines and a billiard room.
Many take-out orders went to the nearby yacht basin and to Roper Hospital,
which had both indigent and private patients. Several young blacks working at
Mike's delivered the orders to the segregated areas such as white and black
medicine. Mike's hamburgers were very popular, but the problem was cooking
them in a small frying pan. At one time I was answering the telephone, taking
orders, racking up the pool table, and trying to cook fifty hamburgers. It was
a mad house.

There was a soft drink machine in front of Mike's store that had two slots
that ran from one side to the other, and in between there was packed ice. If
someone wanted a coke, he would insert a warm one in one slot, and it would
be replaced by a cold one on the other side. The slots often became clogged.
Mike had a long coil with which he would unhook the blockage by passing
the coil down one of the slots. Mike didn't let anyone curse in his shop, but
doing this work he himself cursed a lot. Many doctors came to Mike's for soft
drinks, Nabs, or sandwiches. They often ran a tab that was posted with their
name on a blackboard. They changed the amount on the board each time
they placed an order. One night while I was working, a young doctor came in
who was a little drunk, and he erased the blackboard. I was distressed. The
next morning I met Mike early, and he wondered why I was there. I told him

what happened. Mike was very calm; he reached in his pocket and pulled out a paper with a list of all the amounts that were owed to him. He added the names back on the blackboard and added ten cents to each bill for his effort. You can't fool a Greek.

This Texan was riding in Athens in a cab. He saw a ten-story office building and asked the cab driver, "How long did it take you Greeks to build that thing?" The cab driver answered, "Five years." The Texan said, "We could have done it in three." They next passed a hospital, and the Texan asked the cab driver, "How long did it take you Greeks to build that hospital?" The cab driver answered, "Three years," and the Texan said, "We could have done it in a year and a half." Next they passed a large stadium, and the Texan again asked the cab driver, "How long did it take you Greeks to build that stadium?" The Greek cab driver answered, "I don't know, but it wasn't there yesterday."

Because of my many jobs, I had to study in between my duties as time permitted. In my father's grocery store, customers would get items and come to the cash register to pay while I was studying and reciting my lessons in a low voice. Many thought I had lost my mind. Walking to college each morning, I would review my lessons in a low voice, and many told my parents that I would not acknowledge them. I was determined to learn and use every minute available to study. During 1940-1941, I played college basketball even though I was only five-foot-seven. The other guard was the same height. Our center was six-foot-three and our two forwards were five-foot-eleven. I learned to play basketball in the yard behind our grocery store. Small apple barrels had a circular metal ring around them. I nailed one of these against an outside wall and used it as the basket. This was a problem because I could not practice fast breaks under the basket without hitting the wall. I occasionally went to the playground where there were outside basketball courts. At that time, we shot baskets from our shoulder level and not overhead. Free throws were shot from between our legs. Former basketball players were invited to return for a reunion when the college got a new arena and the last game was played in the old one. They put us in a line beginning with me, since I was the oldest and shortest. The line ran to the current team, which had players as tall as seven feet. A basketball was passed, and the coach at the other end dunked it.

Some college fraternities, even though they have Greek letters, would not accept Greeks, so five Greeks formed their own fraternity—Sigma Epsilon Phi. This was another *through the back door*.

During my third year of college, our physiology professor became ill, and a substitute came from the Medical School's Physiology Department. He was above our level, but as I had read the college physiology book completely, I was able to answer all of his questions. I made ninety-five on his final examination. The other nineteen students did poorly. One day, he asked if I was interested in going to medical school. I said yes, but that I would not be accepted since I was Greek and had no money. It turned out he was on the admissions committee. A few students were accepted from the junior year of college, and I was one of them. The medical school dean tried to block my matriculation, saying that I was too young, had to work, and would not make the grade. At that time I was only eighteen. The mean age today of a first year student is about twenty-four. The dean asked me to stay out and return in two years. I answered that this was a great opportunity and promised I would find a way to pay and study. Again, this was *through the back door*.

I continued to work for Mike during medical school from 8:00 P.M. to midnight closing time. Mike found a freshman student who had dropped out of medical school, and bought his microscope and first-year books. These were most of my expenses as a first-year student. In addition, he agreed to pay my tuition, which I would repay by working for him. At midnight, I'd go home, where I shared a room in the attic with my brother Pat. We did not have air-conditioning, and during the summer it was extremely hot. Often Pat would come in after midnight and talk about the problems he had with his many girlfriends. There was a bar across the street from our home, and we could hear singing and laughter. There was a fire station next door. When it got a call, it would sound a loud alarm. At 2:00 A.M., I would fall asleep. I got up at 7:00 A.M. to open my father's store before going to medical school. My father was always looking for me to work in the store. My mother would hide me so that I could study. My father was a straightforward, honest man who meant well, but he did not understand the rigors of medical school.

Our major course during the freshman year was anatomy and osteology (study of the bones). A maid who worked at times at our home saw a skeleton that I brought home to study; she thought it was her late husband's, and she left us.

Our anatomy professor was Dr. Cyril O'Driscoll, an excellent teacher who relished his role. He was overweight, medium height, and had drooping shoulders. His gray hair was untidy, and his eyebrows were bushy. Gold-rimmed glasses could not obscure his penetrating eyes that often twinkled. He had a turkey gobbler neck (large skin folds hanging under his chin). An unlit pipe was constantly between his lips. A long white coat hung from his drooped shoulders. With dexterity, he would fold his coat to resemble the intestines to the amazement of his students. His language—pungent, pictur-esque, and explicit—was laced with wise sayings and admonitions. He was unpretentious, disciplined, dedicated, religious, loyal, humble, and yet a proud man. If a student hesitated in giving an answer, he would say, "Man, bet your money and sleep in the street." His numerous idiosyncrasies are legendary and will be passed from one generation to another. I remember one Sunday, I was working in the lab, and he came in. "Gentlemen," he said, "You may not be here tomorrow for World War II has just begun." Dr. O'Driscoll gave oral examinations and sat on a high chair and had a clock that he set for fifteen minutes for each student. Two students shared a cadaver. Our cadaver was not prepared properly, and it was spoiled. I had to use strings to represent various nerves. Dr. O'Driscoll asked me to pick out nerves in the armpit. I picked up the strings carefully with a forceps. Saliva from the professor's unlit pipe fell on my cadaver. He spread the saliva with his hand over the strings. He praised me for such a great dissection not realizing that the strings were not real nerves. Another *through the back door*.

Sometimes I would go to the anatomy lab at night to do my dissecting when it was very quiet. One night I had the windows open, and it was raining very hard. I had wrapped a cord around the overhead lamp and my cadaver's hand, so that I could dissect the armpit. After a while, I became sleepy. The wind was very strong, and the lamp began swinging. I was very drowsy, and suddenly the cord gave way, and the cadaver's arm wrapped around my neck. I was frightened and ran home through the rain. Anatomy was one of my favorite first-year subjects.

A young country boy bought a rooster, and on the way home, he saw on the marquee at the theater that John Wayne, his favorite actor, was playing. He stuffed the rooster in his trousers and sat next to a lady in the theater. The rooster became restless, so he unzipped to allow the rooster's head to come out for air. The lady turned to her husband and said, "Honey, look at that." He answered, "You've seen one, you've seen them all." She said, "Yes, but this one is eating my popcorn." Obviously, she did not know her anatomy.

Dr. O'Driscoll gave us a written examination, and one of the major questions was the derivation of the names of bones. Having had Latin and being Greek, I was the only one who answered this question correctly. When he found out I was Greek, he said I had an advantage and that the bone question would be deleted from my exam. Fortunately, he was only kidding. We became great friends and, later, he was one of my patients.

My brother Pat was very curious about my cadaver. I arranged for him to come at night to the lab. Beforehand, I had one of my friends lay on the table, and hid the cadaver under it. My friend was covered with a cloth and raised up when Pat approached. He fainted.

After my first year in medical school, I returned and graduated from the College of Charleston with my class, receiving a BS in medicine. I was first honor in my medical freshman class. Our dean apologized for his earlier doubts, and subsequently, we became great friends. Persistence, determination, and motivation paid off—*through the back door.*

World War II began, and I enlisted in the navy V12 program. It paid a stipend and allowed me to finish medical school. The sophomore year, we studied the basic sciences—physiology, bacteriology, pathology, and pharmacology. We ran many practical experiments. We had a fellow student swallow an inflated condom and recorded his gastric motility. One of our classmate subjects swallowed the inflated condom, and after the experiment his partner pulled it out before deflating it. He shrieked loudly, but fortunately, his stomach and esophagus were not injured.

Clinical studies began in our junior year. Taking care of patients for the first time was interesting and rewarding. We had to present patients to our attending physicians and report laboratory studies, many of which we performed ourselves. Some schools today integrate the curriculum of the basic science and clinical year. The students enjoy this for they have patients even in their freshman year.

During my junior year, I was on an elevator in the old Charleston Roper Hospital. The elevator was operated by James, a very dedicated worker. In spite of a stroke with partial paralysis, he ran the elevator. It was like a steel cage and had a cable with a wheel that James had to turn to get to the various floors. That day, a very distinguished man from New York got on the elevator. James noticed that the man had a paralysis similar to his. He asked the man if he was going to see the brain surgeon, Dr. Frederick Kredel. The man said, "Yes," and James mentioned that Dr. Kredel had operated on him because after his stroke he had frequent epileptic seizures. Since his surgery, James said, he had no more seizures. Just as he said that, he had a grand mal seizure that shook the elevator.

The New York man looked in despair. I tried to keep James from biting his tongue. Dr. Kredel was tall and had a distinguished appearance, with gray hair and a moustache. He was a bright, soft-spoken person. He seldom wore dress clothes and often was seen in his operating scrubs (outfits).

Dr. Kredel performed experimental brain vascularization operations. He dissected a muscle from the face with its blood supply and sutured it to the side of the brain where the stroke occurred with the hope it would revascularize that area. To this day, I don't know if the man from New York ever had the procedure.

Speaking about elevators, this is a story I heard.

The devil was operating the elevator from hell to heaven. The elevator kept breaking down. God said, "If you don't operate it better, I will sue you." The devil said, "No way. There are no lawyers in heaven."

The old Roper Hospital was an architectural pearl. Besides the elevator, it had many old features. Unfortunately, Roper Hospital was torn down and replaced with a parking garage. James eventually could not work any longer and sold peanuts at the old Market Place in downtown Charleston. Each Christmas he brought me a bag of peanuts.

A senior student who was serving an externship (a position students could get to prepare for their internship) at the private St. Francis Hospital across from the medical school, had to return home because of illness in his family. He could not find anyone else to cover for him and asked me. I had finished my sophomore year and had just begun examining patients. I accepted, and the first day, I was called to the delivery room. During World War II, many doctors could not get there in time, and students had to do the deliveries. I had never seen a delivery but knew how to put on my facemask, gown, and gloves. Sister Maria, a Catholic nun, was giving the anesthesia. She realized that I was inexperienced and began describing how a baby was delivered by one of the popular obstetricians in town. I followed her suggestions, and the baby was delivered without difficulty. Sister Maria and I became great friends. She became head of the hospital and, later, one of my patients.

Two rednecks at a football game were sitting behind two nuns who wore large hats that were part of their religious habits. The rednecks could not see well, and one said, "I'm going to North Dakota because there are few Catholics there." The other one said, "I'm going to Utah because there are even fewer Catholics there." One of the nuns turned and said, "Why don't you go to hell. There are no Catholics there."

One day they called me to a room to pronounce a patient dead. I ran up to the floor and entered the room; I saw nuns on their knees, and a priest giving last rites. I did not know what to do, so I got on my knees too. One of the attending physicians was passing by and saw me. The next day during his lecture, he said that he saw one of their classmates praying to bring a dead patient back to life.

During my junior year, I developed tendonitis from playing handball. I could not write and had to take my examinations orally. This was exceedingly difficult, but I passed. One of the professors I got to know very well was Dr. Horace Smithy. Dr. Smithy was very muscular and tanned. He had an intense interest in athletics, including participating in professional baseball and boxing. In addition, he was an avid golfer. He had a great facility in teaching medical students, nurses, and house staff. He was internationally known for performing one of the first open-heart surgeries on the mitral valve. He had aortic stenosis (narrowing of the aortic valve) and was working on surgical experiments to open the valve. Once he thought he had the procedure developed, he went to Johns Hopkins to have Dr. Blalock, a famous cardiac surgeon, perform the surgery on him. Dr. Smithy was going to operate on a man with aortic stenosis and Dr. Smithy's body size, and Dr. Blalock was to observe. If successful, he would then perform the surgery on Dr. Smithy. Unfortunately, the patient's heart stopped during anesthesia before the surgery started. The patient could not be resuscitated, and Dr. Smithy returned home disappointed. One month later at the age of thirty-two, he died of congestive heart failure.

Dr. Smithy was very tough on students. During one of his classes he brought in a patient with a swelling on the left side of his face. His students examined the man but could not make a diagnosis. I raised my hand, and Dr. Smithy said, "Smarty, come on down and feel it." I did, and I told him it was a stone in the parotid duct—the correct diagnosis. What Dr. Smithy did not know is that I had the identical problem when I was very young. My face had become swollen, and I ran a high fever. The doctor came and told my mother to use hot compresses, but my fever raged on, and the swelling got worse. I did not sleep for several days, and then one night, the stone passed through the duct, and the swelling ended.

My senior year, I had an externship at St. Francis and delivered over 100 babies. This reminds me of a story of a mother who had a twenty-five-pound baby.

All her neighbors came by to see this huge baby. One of the neighbors came back later to see how the baby was doing. The mother said the baby was very well and now weighed fifteen pounds. The lady asked her how he could be well having lost ten pounds. The mother said, "Oh, he was circumcised."

Before we graduated we had to perform twenty-five home deliveries, usually on indigent patients. We drove with a resident physician to the expectant mother's home, and he checked to be certain that it was not a breech delivery. Breech is a presentation of the buttocks or feet of the fetus instead of the head. One time I remained all night with my patient, and she did not deliver.

Finally, at 7:00 A.M. I told her daughter that I would go to the drugstore to get a cup of coffee and something to eat. I had just begun eating when the daughter came running and said the baby's arm was coming out. The resident had missed the breech. Fortunately, I was able to deliver her without complication. Except for this case, many students wondered why I came home very early after most of my deliveries. The answer was simple—many of these patients' grandmothers were midwives. I would sit on the porch and peep through the window. The grandmother would have them stand and strain, and they would deliver. I had to run to the room and catch the baby and placenta. One night I had a delivery above a nightclub. The lady's husband was a sergeant in the army and would not leave the room because he thought I was too young. Naturally, I became nervous, and when the baby delivered, I dropped the baby on the bed. The husband came toward me and said, "I knew you didn't know what you were doing." I was very fast and stated, "You know you have to drop them, so they will begin breathing." Another *through the back door* experience.

Just after the delivery I heard footsteps and a person calling for the doctor because there was a shooting in the nightclub. I went down and saw a man who was obviously dead on the floor and another man with a gun. I ran outside, got into my old Ford, and went to the police station for help.

Often, mothers wanted us to give their babies a last name. Some of our class gave the names of prominent downtown citizens. The dean became aware of this and told us if this continued we would not graduate.

One of my friends is so ugly that at birth the doctor slapped his mother. Every time I see him I wonder why we can't have retroactive abortion.

I often played tricks on the nurses, and one night I went to the dining room at midnight to have a cup of coffee. One of them paid me back by slipping a heavy laxative in my coffee. The next day I had diarrhea so bad I had to take intravenous fluids.

This reminds me of a young doctor who went to observe an elder doctor. The first patient who came in had a cough. The old doctor wrote a prescription for a laxative. The young doctor asked him, "Why would you give a laxative for a cough?" The elder doctor answered, "If he coughs, he will know about it."

The externship at St. Francis Hospital gave me a world of experience that paid off during my regular internship. I learned that you should listen to a patient's story and perform a good physical examination. Physicians sometimes forget this.

A lady called the information desk of a hospital and asked how a patient named Sarah Brown was doing. The operator said that Sarah Brown was in room 325, and she would connect her with the nurse's station. The nurse said that Sarah Brown was great; in fact, she was walking up and down the hall, and probably would go home tomorrow. The lady said that is the greatest news I have heard in a long time, and she went on and on. The nurse said your enthusiasm suggests that you are a relative or good friend. She said, "Neither. I am Sarah Brown in room 325, and no one tells me a thing."

During the externship I often had to perform laboratory studies on urine and specimens of feces.

A patient, who was hard of hearing, went to a doctor with his wife. The doctor examined him and said, "I would like a specimen of your urine, feces, and semen." The patient turned to his wife and said, "What did he say?" The wife answered, "He wants to see your shorts."

The most interesting student rotation was to the emergency room. It is hard to describe what we saw. One day a man was brought in bleeding in the groin. As soon as he arrived he vomited up something bad. The pathology report said it was one partially digested testicle. It turned out this man was caught having an affair with another man's wife. The husband took a knife and cut out one of his testicles and made him eat it. I was told that ten years later he did the same thing, and the husband cut out the man's other testicle.

Another time a student who the night before had been at a party, came in with blood in his urine. He said he tried to make love with a young woman, but since he was drunk, he could not perform. She pushed a candle up his penis hoping to produce an erection.

Because of the war, I finished medical school in three years without a vacation. During my junior and senior years, I was number one in my class. Bernard Baruch gave our graduation address, and I was honored to receive the first honor award from him. The Baruch Auditorium was donated to the medical school by Bernard Baruch in memory of his father, Simon Baruch, a physician.

My greatest desire was to become a physician. Today our youth have many opportunities, and they should take advantage of them. I had obstacles to overcome, but again, because of motivation, determination, and persistency, I got *through the back door.*

CHAPTER 3

INTERNSHIP, NAVY, INTERNAL MEDICINE, AND CARDIOLOGY FELLOWSHIP

The Making of a Doctor

As first-honor graduate from the medical school, I had the choice for internship in many great institutions. However, because of World War II many hospitals reduced available positions. A friend who was a resident at Jersey City Medical Center visited Charleston and convinced me to apply there. I was accepted. Another *through the back door* experience.

All internships were of the rotating type on different services such as surgery and medicine. My internship was great. We did many procedures since attending physicians were scarce because of World War II. Initially I wanted to be surgeon. Jersey City was my first experience north of the Mason Dixon Line. I found that people all over the Unites States of America are wonderful.

This was the first time I saw snow. I said to the nurses, "Isn't it wonderful that all this cotton is coming down from heaven?"

The medical center was well managed. Mayor Hague of Jersey City made it a high priority. We had private rooms and baths, and a great dining room. Many of the waitresses thought I was a young boy, though I was twenty-two. On election day, the food improved considerably. Instead of hot dogs ("tube steaks"), we got real steaks. We got as many of our patients as possible to the polls.

Mayor Hague would not allow dancing or drinking in the same club. For both we had to go to Union City. I often took the elevated train to New York to see shows. Sometimes, returning, I fell asleep and ended up on the train that stopped at Hoboken. I had to wait at least an hour before catching another train to Jersey City.

We had to work two straight days before taking a half day off. On an off day, I once skinned my leg playing baseball, and it became infected. Penicillin had just then become available, but it had to be given by intramuscular injection every four hours by a doctor. Ten days after the injection, I began to itch all over. It continued for several days. No one knew the cause. I was even sent to a psychiatrist who thought I suffered from an anxiety syndrome. Speaking about psychiatrists...

A blind man was crossing the street when his dog peed on him. He reached in his pocket and gave the dog a biscuit. A psychiatrist saw him and said, "That's the worst thing you can do—rewarding the dog for what he did." The blind man said, "Look, I know what I am doing. I want to know where his head is, so I can kick him in the ass."

My itching didn't go way, and I began to have hives. My joints became swollen. I was given starch baths with a nurse holding my head above water so I could sleep. A young internist who had just set up his private practice made a diagnosis of late penicillin reaction. Fortunately, it cleared.

After nine months of internship, I went into the navy as a lieutenant (junior grade). I was ordered to the naval hospital in Dublin, Georgia, for indoctrination. The only way to get there was by train to Macon and from there by bus to Dublin. On the bus I met two young ladies who were returning home from college for a weekend. While at the naval hospital I got a call from the mayor of Dublin. It turned out that one of the two girls was his daughter, and he asked me to visit him at his home for lunch. Sunday morning, the mayor drove up in a chauffeured car. He was wearing a white suit. My friends watched in amazement as I got into the back seat with the mayor's daughter and her roommate. We had a great lunch, except that the mayor kept taking out his false teeth, which seemed to rattle when he chewed.

An elderly man and his wife went to a restaurant. He said to the waiter, "We share everything. We each would like a five-ounce hamburger and twelve french fries. After a while, the waiter returned to the table and saw that the wife had eaten everything, but the man had not touched his food. He asked, "What is wrong?" The man said, "Didn't I tell you we share everything? I am waiting for her false teeth."

A retired minister was invited by a young priest to preach at his church. That morning, in a rush, the old man forgot to put in his false teeth. The young priest said, "Don't worry. I will take care of it." Not long after, he returned with a perfectly good set of teeth. "It's wonderful this parish has a dentist," said the old man. The priest answered, "Oh, it was not our dentist who helped you out—it was our mortician."

Dublin was a small, one-block town. Its naval hospital was well built and well equipped. In fact, it is now a Veterans Hospital, and I was a consultant there later. My indoctrination there was very tough. We had to get up at 5:00 A.M. and, under the direction of a former FBI agent, we jogged five miles. Then, wearing a pack, we jumped into a swimming pool. Some of the doctors were old and out of condition. After they complained our jogging stopped.

The hospital administrator asked what service I would like, and I said surgery. The navy, however, assigned me to internal medicine. I worked in a patient ward with suspected acute rheumatic fever cases. The first day on rounds I saw that only a few who actually had rheumatic fever, while others had late penicillin allergic symptoms similar to those I had earlier. Some of the patients had venereal diseases and were given penicillin. This again was a *through the back door* moment. Patients with rheumatic fever often have heart complications, and this was my first exposure to cardiology.

A family had a large heart with flowers built for a cardiologist's funeral. After the eulogy, the heart opened, the casket was rolled in, and the doors closed. Suddenly there was loud laughter. Everyone turned around, and the person laughing stated, "Excuse me. I was thinking of my funeral. I am a gynecologist." A person next to him fainted. He was a proctologist.

Our chief of medicine was from Detroit and asked me to present a patient who presumably had pernicious anemia to our morning medical conference. The night before, I went to check on the patient. A patient in a bed next to him said that it was not pernicious anemia. "He walks barefooted on red clay and has hookworms," he said. I checked the patient's stool, and it was positive for hookworms. The next morning my chief lectured on pernicious anemia. When I told him that his patient had hookworms, I thought he would send me overseas. I had embarrassed and confused him.

A crossed-eyed judge was presented with three crossed-eye witnesses. He looked at the first and asked, "What is your name?" The second one said, "John Doe." He looked at the third and said, "I didn't ask you," and the first said, "I didn't say anything."

It was very hot during the month of July in Dublin. Gnats or "no-see-ums" were vicious. Several small children developed eye infections, and one child's eye had to be removed. One night I was called to the delivery room to see a commander's wife in labor. The obstetrician was not available, and the first-call physician was an ear, nose, and throat specialist. My past experience paid off. The delivery turned out to be very simple.

After six weeks of indoctrination, I returned to Charleston, where I received orders to go to San Diego. I first went to the Balboa Naval Hospital and from there to Coronado, where marines were in training. The navy medical corps provided doctors and corpsmen to the marines. We were housed in the Hotel Del Coronado, a beautiful resort hotel. At that time, one had to cross the Bay of Coronado by ferry. On the ferry, I met Johnny Misoyianis, a childhood friend who had enlisted in the navy. We had dinner together and enjoyed talking about our families. At Coronado, the marines trained for overseas duty. After one month I was sent to a large Quonset hut with about 100 other physicians waiting on further orders. After several days, I decided to go to San Francisco with a few friends. Just as I was about to leave, my name was called to report for overseas duty.

Our ship was a converted luxury liner taken over by the navy. It took almost a full day to load 5,000 marines. I was in a stateroom with two other passengers—an army major and a navy lieutenant commander. We got only two meals a day—one at 8:00 A.M. and another at 8:00 P.M. My two roommates convinced me that I should check with the ship's doctors because they certainly would need help and, by volunteering, I would have access to the mess hall. I could bring them back some food. The ship's doctors welcomed me with open arms and gave me my first assignment. I was to give short arm inspections to the 5,000 marines. I sat in a chair and instructed each marine "to skin it (his penis) back and milk it down." I detected 200 cases of gonorrhea. No—this was not another *through the back door* moment.

A man in a drugstore asked for aspirin, Exlax, and a pack of condoms. A person behind him said, "Why do you do it if it makes you sick?"

Our ship made it to Hawaii, and no one there seemed to know where I was to go. I was sent to a large Quonset hut where there were many other doctors. Eventually I was assigned to an landing ship tank (LST) as a flagship for smaller landing craft. The LST had so many problems that, after much confusion, I was temporarily assigned to the dispensary at Pearl Harbor. The Pearl Harbor Dispensary took care of the navy, the marines, and their civilian employees and their families. I was one of the few of its physicians who had completed an internship in general medicine. Many of the others were specialists and glad to have someone who would take care of general complaints. I cherished the opportunity because at this point I had seen very few patients. The commanding officer demanded much of his physicians. He was impressed by my eagerness and made me head physician of the dispensary above others who had higher rank. This gave me many perks, such as a Jeep that allowed me to travel around the island. After several months, I was supposed to go back to the marines, but my commanding officer arranged for me to stay at the dispensary with some duties at the Aiea Naval Hospital.

Bill Zeller, one of the doctors, and I became great friends and roommates. He was married and had two children. A letter from his wife mentioned that his children were sick. He was depressed, and I drove him to Honolulu to Trader Vic's, a famous bar. There he introduced me to a Zombie, a refreshing but potent drink with several different strengths of rum. Only two were allowed per customer. However, I talked the bartender into allowing me to have more, telling him my friend would do the driving. Before the evening was over, I even danced with a hula girl.

A young soldier wrote his father and said, "I can't tell you where I am, but yesterday I shot a polar bear." Several months later he wrote his father again and said "I can't tell you where I am, but last night I danced with a hula girl. A few months later he wrote, "The doctor says I should have danced with the polar bear and shot the hula girl."

On the way back to our quarters, we stopped and had a hamburger. My next recollection was 2:00 A.M. when I awoke with Bill slapping my back. I was vomiting in my sleep. I thought that it was the hamburger that made me sick not the Zombies.

Bill became a psychiatrist and spent many years at the famous Hartford Retreat psychiatric institution (now the Institute of Living).

Another story is that of an individual who went to Fifth Avenue in New York to get the best psychiatrist. He went into the waiting room and saw that it was well furnished and decorated. No one was there, though. There were two doors. Over one was a sign reading Male. Over the other, Female. He went through the Male door and entered another well decorated and furnished room, but no one was there either. In this room were two doors labeled Introverts and Extroverts. He went through the Introvert door and again was in an empty room. This had two doors with signs: Those with income under $50,000 and the other, Those with income over $50,000. He went through the under $50,000 door and found himself back on Fifth Avenue.

The war ended, and I had at two months to go before I completed my tour of duty. Since I was single and Greek, I tried to get an assignment in Greece. I had never been to my parents' native country. Our commanding officer at the dispensary was notified of this and immediately said he was sending me to Oakland, California, with several brain-injury cases. He said I was too interested in medicine and that if I accepted an assignment to Greece I'd be obligated for three years. I'd be stuck in the navy just as he had, and end up as an administrator rather than a physician. Yet one more *through the back door* moment.

After delivering the brain-injury patients, I spent one month in San Francisco before I was discharged from the navy. San Francisco is a wonderful city, and I thought of remaining there. Specialized training at that time was much better on the East Coast, however. I was accepted to return for surgery training at the New Jersey Medical Center. In Hawaii, I had met a radiologist from the University of Pennsylvania, and he mentioned that the best training was at Philadelphia General Hospital (PGH). Hahnemann, Jefferson, Women's Hospital of Philadelphia, University of Pennsylvania, and Temple University had services at PGH. While waiting to return to Jersey City, I received a call from my radiologist friend telling me that I was accepted at PGH. After much thought, I canceled the Jersey City appointment and went to Philadelphia. Philadelphia General Hospital was a wonderful place to specialize. However, I could not start my specialty because I did not have a Pennsylvania State license and to get one cost $200, which I did not have. I was told that I could take the Pennsylvania State examination for $5 but had to complete pediatrics and ob-gyn rotations, which I had not had during my internship at Jersey City. Therefore, I took two months rotation on these services.

During this time, I became interested in electrocardiography (ECG) reading and went daily to the ECG station. Dr. Franklin Fetter was the assistant superintendent of PGH, a great doctor and a wonderful person who later became dean of the Medical School of South Carolina. During my two months of internship rotations, I found that I liked diagnosis better than surgery. I asked Dr. Fetter if I could change to internal medicine. He was amazed since I had been accepted for surgery from a field of so many candidates. He said I could change to internal medicine if I started as a resident in the emergency room and took care of the firemen and policemen. This turned out to be a great rotation, and I praised it so much that they added it to the internal medicine rotation. I had an office in the emergency room and mounted electrocardiograms for one of the attending physicians who was writing a textbook.

One day Dr. Fetter sent a beautiful redhead to my office with a note, "Do what you can for this young lady." I asked her what was her problem. She said, "I am getting messages from heaven." I asked, "How are these messages coming?" She said, "From five wires to my head." I told her to bend with her head over my desk. I had a large pair of scissors that I used to cut ECGs for mounting and asked her to count as I cut the wires. All the nurses and interns were wondering what I was doing. After she counted to five she said the messages were gone. I told her to return to Dr. Fetter. Later, when Dr. Fetter became dean of our medical school, I reminded him of this.

My interest in cardiology became much stronger because of the firemen and policemen that I took care of. Many in these occupations have blockages of the coronary arteries and suffer heart attacks. I became friends with many of them, and they gave me a lot of perks such as tickets to Philadelphia Eagles and the University of Pennsylvania football games. I also could park anywhere in Philadelphia without getting a ticket. At PGH, I met many interesting doctors. One of my interns, Dottie, was married to an all-American football player, Pete Pehos, of Indiana. He came to play with the Philadelphia Eagles.

After a few months at PGH, I decided to go to downtown Philadelphia for the first time. I was waiting outside the University of Pennsylvania when a student on my service at PGH asked that I join him at a fraternity party. At first I was reluctant but then agreed to go for a short time. Some were dancing, and I saw a beautiful young lady whom I thought I had previously seen. I tagged her male partner. At that time, tagging was thought proper. I tried to convince her that I had seen her before. A month earlier my parents came through Philadelphia, and we went to church. This young lady was sitting in front of me. I tried to impress her with my southern charm, but she ignored me. I told her my name was Pete Gazes, "like gazing at the stars." She really thought I was a jerk. She was very popular and was voted queen at that night's affair. I kept tagging her for a dance. While dancing she invited many to a party at her home, and I invited myself. And thus I met Athena, *through the back door* because of my persistence.

At the party, I met her brother, Pete, and her parents. After many phone calls, I convinced her to go out with me. Our living quarters at PGH were across the corner from the Philadelphia convention center. Athena and her friends were going to a Frank Sinatra concert, and she said that after this she would meet me. I dressed up and told all my friends to watch from the window to see this "doll." I waited, but she never showed up. Later, Athena confessed she saw me but went on to a drugstore. There she told her friends, "I stood up Dr. Gazes." In the neighboring booth several nurses jumped up and said, "You mean you stood up Dr. Gazes? None of us would have done that."

Finally, Athena agreed to go with me to the musical *Kismet*, provided her mother could come along. At the theater her mother sat between us and fell asleep. I had to reach across her to hold Athena's hand.

I frequently visited Athena at Drexel College. Our torrid relationship began in September and ended up with an engagement in November and marriage in June. One day I saw a large picture of Athena in a portrait studio. She was not aware that it was being displayed. I asked her to go with me to see a picture of a monkey. She did, and that was how I gave her the nickname of Monkey.

My father-in-law went all out and gave us a big wedding with a seated dinner for about 200 people. My best man was a good friend from Charleston. One of the nurses from PGH recommended Mohonk Lake Inn for our honeymoon. This was just north of Poughkeepsie, New York. When we arrived at the Poughkeepsie station we were met by a horse and buggy that carried us to the inn. There were several elderly couples in the same buggy. The ride through the mountains was beautiful. The inn was magnificent and old as the hills. The elevator was pulled up by ropes. Our room had two single beds with a fireplace in between. I immediately went to the desk and asked for a double bed. None was available. I next asked where the bar was and what entertainment there was. It turned out the inn was run by Quakers, and the only nighttime activities were prayer meetings and Bible studies.

I had committed for the week and could not book a room in New York City. However, we stayed for the week and enjoyed every moment. Athena convinced me to go horseback riding, which I had never done before. The horse and I did not get along well. My behind became very sore from going up and down on the saddle. That night when I walked into the dining room with my legs bowed, an elderly couple looked at me and one of them said out loud, "Newlyweds." I pointed to my legs and said, "Horseback riding." Speaking of horseback riding…

This minister was driving with his wife and saw a man on horseback, and he said he would give a sermon the coming Sunday on horseback riding. His wife said you have never done horseback riding, and I am not going to hear you make a fool of yourself. That Sunday on his way to church without his wife, he saw a girl in a bikini jogging. He decided to change his sermon to sex. Monday morning, a parishioner saw the minister's wife and said, "I am certainly glad that you did not come to church to hear your husband's sermon on Sunday." His wife said, "I know. I told him not to preach that topic because he only tried it twice and both times he fell off backwards."

I understand that the Mohonk Lake Inn is still there, and we hope, if we reach ninety, to return. The area has changed since our marriage on June 1, 1947, and there are now many inns there. Hopefully, we can find the right one.

When we came back from our honeymoon, Athena's relatives were still celebrating the wedding. This was the Greek custom.

After marriage, Greeks often live with their in-laws, but we could not live with ours because they were still living with theirs.

My two years in internal medicine were wonderful. Several medical schools in Philadelphia had patients (services) at PGH. I was fortunate to have one of the better ones, the Temple service. My chief was Dr. Thomas Durant, a kind, considerate person and an excellent diagnostician. Physicians came from everywhere to round (examine patients) with him, as many as thirty at one time. He made separate rounds with me. If I presented a case, he would say that the findings I described were not present today. That was his way of not embarrassing me.

The following is one of the sketches for the person least likely to have coronary disease (taking into account a number of studies and statistical reports) that Dr. Durant often quoted. I updated this with recent new finding.

An effeminate municipal worker or an embalmer completely lacking in physical and mental alertness, without drive, ambition or competitive spirit, who has never attempted to meet a deadline of any kind. A man with poor appetite, subsisting on fruits and vegetables, laced with olive, canola, and fish oils, detesting tobacco, spurning ownership of radio, TV, or a motor car, with a full head of hair, scrawny and unathletic in appearance, yet constantly straining his puny muscles by exercise. Low in income, blood pressure, blood sugar, uric acid, and cholesterol, who has been taking nicotinic acid, statin drugs, antioxidants, aspirin, and long-term anticoagulant therapy ever since his prophylactic castration.

After my internal medicine rotation, I began my cardiology fellowship. Again, I was blessed with two wonderful and knowledgeable head physicians, the late Dr. Thomas McMillan and the late Dr. Samuel Bellett. They were a good team because Dr. McMillan was very calm and Dr. Bellett was a driver and spastic. I gained from Dr. McMillan's clinical acumen and Dr. Bellett's research regime. We published many articles together on the effects of potassium on the electrocardiogram (ECG).

During my cardiac fellowship, Dr. Bellett hired Harry Gold, a laboratory chemist, to perform the chemistries for our research. Harry was an unassuming, quiet individual who noticeably lost a lot of weight. He was very dedicated to his work and practically lived in the hospital. He performed lab studies for us even when they did not pertain to our research. After my fellowship and return to Charleston, I was amazed to learn that he was arrested as a Soviet spy. He had acted as a "courier" for a ring during the Manhattan Project (development of the atomic bomb). In 1950 Klaus Fuchs, a German physicist who worked at the Los Alamos Laboratory in New Mexico during World War II, passed information about the atom bomb to Harry Gold. One of my associates at Philadelphia General Hospital said that Gold was arrested in Philadelphia after the FBI had interviewed 3,000 chemists in the New York and Philadelphia areas. After his apartment was searched, he confessed. They found a map of New Mexico with an area marked where he had exchanged information. Gold was a key witness in the trials of Ethel and Julius Rosenberg and Daniel Greenglass. All were found guilty. Gold was given a thirty-year sentence in 1951. In 1966 he was paroled, and he died in 1973.

Athena and I had one lovely daughter while in Philadelphia. We had a small apartment that was in walking distance of the hospital. One day Athena called me at the hospital to say she had cooked my favorite meal. When I got home I found very hard white balls on my plate. I thought they were mothballs. She could not understand why I did not eat. They were hominy balls and not the grits we southerners like.

Our apartment rent was $50.00 a month. At the time I was making about $90.00 a month. I moonlighted to make ends meet. The main emergency room in Philadelphia was at PGH. Very sick, indigent patients were referred there, and I had to do the screening. On many nights, my phone rang constantly. In addition Athena contributed by modeling hats at Gimbels department store in Philadelphia.She also won a television which were rare at that time and very expensive

After completion of my fellowship, I was offered a faculty position at the University of Pennsylvania. Dr. Walton, my professor of pharmacology at the medical school, with whom I had done research, convinced me to return to Charleston because there was no certified cardiologist there. After one year at the Medical School of South Carolina, I was not earning enough to support my family. I remained part time at the school and went into private practice. At the medical school several internists did all of the cardiology work. They did not allow me to see patients or read electrocardiograms.

Internship, internal medicine, and a cardiology fellowship rounded my career. Because of my training, cardiology was my future in medicine. Today, students in medicine have many options. They may go into general practice, become a professor, a researcher, or specialize in many fields. I went *through the back door* to become a cardiologist.

CHAPTER 4
PART TIME AT THE MEDICAL SCHOOL AND IN-TOWN PRIVATE PRACTICE

Phenomenal Work

Opening an office was very expensive. First, I acquired office space next to a friend's drugstore. He agreed not to charge rent at least for one year. The place was a large open space that needed partitions and painting. My next-door neighbor was a carpenter and willingly helped with no charge. Another neighbor was a major in the army and was a good electrician. We worked together. Next, I needed equipment and waiting room furniture. Old chairs and sofas from our family furnished a comfortable waiting area. I went to the bank to borrow money for my medical equipment. I was turned down because I had no collateral. They apparently did not want to invest in a young doctor. Fortunately, a General Electric salesman came by who sold electrocardiographic machines and an upright fluoroscope (a device used for examining the motion of deep structures by X-ray). At that time there was no one in Charleston with experience in fluoroscopy of the heart. General Electric (GE) sold me the equipment with no down payment and no monthly charge. I could pay as my practice developed. GE called a company in Charlotte, North Carolina, that paid my expenses to visit them. They had a large salesroom with examination tables, sterilizers, and other equipment. They gave me the same arrangement for payment that I had with General

Electric.   My friend Mr. Garbis gave me a leather doctor's bag that I still have. I paid the two companies back in a short time. This was another example of *through the back door.*

Private practice was very demanding since I was the only cardiologist in town and had no one to share night calls. Initially, family doctors did not refer patients to me because I was an unknown quantity. One day a young man came to see me with a rapid heart beat (tachycardia). It turned out to be a very simple problem, and I stopped his tachycardia by putting pressure on the carotid sinus in his neck. The sinus is a dilated portion of the carotid artery containing nerves in its walls that if stimulated slow the heart rate. He was very impressed, for other doctors would have put him in bed for several days and given him sedatives. He had a peculiar quirk. During an attack, he would yell out loud. After he saw me, every time he had an attack he yelled and said, "Call Dr. Gazes." He'd do this in movie theaters, in church, and in other places. Soon everyone in town knew me. This and one other thing jump-started my practice. A popular internist called me one Christmas Day to see a patient who had a heart attack and then developed a rapid, irregular heart rhythm that could not be controlled. It was something I had previously seen, and the treatment I recommended worked. Now I had an "in" and received many consultations from this internist. Another thing that helped me through the back door was reading electrocardiograms. Several internists read electro-cardiograms in private hospitals and would not allow me to participate. Since I was now receiving many consults, I asked the physicians who referred patients to me if I could read their electrocardiograms. Soon I was reading more of these than ever.

I met many interesting patients. This and the fact that I could follow their progress made my practice very rewarding. One day my secretary asked that I see a patient who was brought in and placed on a table in a back room. Unfortunately he was dead, and the people who brought him were gone. He had no identification on him. This was a problem because the only way out was through my waiting room where there were several patients. For a new doctor, this would not look good. All my major equipment was in the room where the dead man had been put. The examination table had a cloth skirt that my wife had made. My secretary and I placed the dead patient under the table. The skirt hid him nicely. I saw my waiting patients quickly and then called the coroner. Another *through the back door* experience.

On another occasion, an elderly man whom I had just seen went into the waiting room and in a loud voice told his wife what I told him. He had asked what he could safely lift and I told him, "Nothing heavier than folding money or women."

Effie La Brasca, a friend, had a restaurant near my office. Any time a person did not eat his entire meal she thought he was sick and sent him to me for an examination. She was a patient too and often sat in my waiting room passing around high-fat biscuits to those who were on a diet.

I made a great mistake in my office setup. My office was next to the waiting room. One day I took a patient's history, a man who had many complaints. I asked about his sex life. He jumped out of the chair and began yelling, "That *is* the problem." He proceeded to describe his sexual activities, which were varied and interesting. My secretary kept buzzing me, for everyone in the waiting room could hear and some were becoming hysterical. Since then I always advise doctors starting in practice to keep a healthy distance between their office and the waiting room.

The only car I could afford then was a secondhand, black Dodge. One day after office hours I could not find my car. My secretary said that Mr. P.O. Mead, a patient, traded my car in for a beautiful silver station wagon. This was the greatest gift that I had ever received from a patient. I thanked P.O., and he said that my old Dodge looked like a hearse, and if I made a house call to him, people would think he had died. Mr. Mead was a wealthy lumberman and a very shrewd businessman. He was very charitable and often he would ask if I had a patient who could not afford hospitalization or needed private nurses. He would anonymously take care of the bill. At one of his plantations at Christmas, he filled a large room with clothing and gifts that were given to the poor.

I gave many lectures around the state and elsewhere in the southeast. My practice became very large, and I hardly had time to see my family. We had two more daughters and in order to get to know them, I took them with me on Saturdays by airplane to consultations in a Savannah hospital. They loved the plane ride immensely. They got to know many nurses who gave them a lot of attention and cookies.

A Catholic priest was on an airplane, and the stewardess asked him if he wanted a drink, and he said, "A Scotch and water." Not realizing that the man sitting next to him was a Baptist minister, she asked if he wanted a drink, too. The minister looked up and said, "I would rather commit adultery." The Catholic priest gave his drink back and said, "I didn't realize we had a choice."

Yeaman's Hall is a resort north of Charleston where many VIPs have homes. It has an outstanding golf course and clubhouse. The attending physician at

Yeaman's Hall called a consultant in Philadelphia to come down and see a member of the Drexel family. I had worked with this consultant, and he told the Yeaman's Hall physician to call me. After this, I got his referrals. After I examined his patients, he wanted me to go over the evaluation and treatment with him, and not them. It wasn't long before the patients realized this and began to see me directly. Another patient was treated for endocarditis (an infected heart valve) for four weeks with penicillin in New York. After arriving at Yeaman's Hall, he began having fever again, and I was called in for consultation. He refused to come to my office, so I went to Yeaman's Hall. I could find no evidence of valvular disease or endocarditis. On questioning, he said that doctors would not listen to his major complaint. He had pain during bowel movements. I gave him a rectal examination. I found a large abscess. It was amazing to me that such wealthy patients often got the worst treatment.

My part-time hours at the medical school were spent primarily in clinical pharmacology with Dr. Walton. As I mentioned before, cardiology was practiced by several internists who did allow me to participate. I taught the use of cardiovascular drugs and also was involved in the supervision of students who were candidates for a PhD in pharmacology. At night I met with them to evaluate animal experiments. Many of our results were published in peer journals. We described the use of sympathomimetic amine (stimulating drugs) in cardiogenic shock (blood pressure drop at very low levels inadequate to support life) and also found for the first time that nitroglycerin in addition to dilating the coronaries would dilate the peripheral vessels.

At 3:00 A.M. one morning, Dr. Tom Darby and I were pulling equipment down the street to study a patient with cardiogenic shock at St. Francis Hospital. A policeman thought we had stolen the equipment. It took awhile to convince him that we were going to study a patient.

Many interesting things happened during my private practice. I was called one night to see a very important Charleston man at his downtown office. His son greeted me when I got there, but his father was already dead, and he was nude. The son was concerned because his mother was on the way, and his father's mistress was still with the body. We ushered her out and then began dressing him. It was not easy because he weighed over 200 pounds. Tying his bow tie was a chore. I knew how to do it, but not without looking in a mirror. The son held him in a sitting position with a mirror in front and I got behind and successfully tied it just before his mother arrived.

Another time a patient called me at 2:00 A.M., who said that his wife had a severe headache. They had just returned from a party and were having sex. Instead of KY jelly lubricant he used nitrol (nitroglycerin) ointment. It gave her the headache. I became interested in nitrol ointment several years ago. First, I did not think it would work, but Dr. Walton said it was absorbed well through the skin. One night I rubbed it on my skin and got a severe, pounding headache. I used it on many patients who had nocturnal angina, and it reduced my night calls significantly. Today, instead of the ointment on waxed paper being placed on the chest, there are nice clean patches (like a Band-aid) for patients with coronary artery disease.

A well-dressed young man came to see me once. He was hesitant to talk and finally he showed me his arm. There was a large red bump on his forearm. This was a puzzle, for it was not warm as an infection would be. The man was a newlywed and suffered from premature ejaculation, which upset his wife. A friend in the army gave him some procaine (a local anesthetic) to inject at the base of his penis to slow ejaculation. He first injected some in his forearm and he noted it deadened the area. Next he injected his penis. Soon after this, a red area occurred in both places. I immediately referred him to a urologist.

Another time I was running late in my office, and I was so tired. Just before leaving at about 9:00 P.M., a Greek from a nearby restaurant came in because of high blood pressure. He could speak very little English. I wanted to weigh him and told him to step on the scales. *Zigizo*, Greek for weighing a person, sounds similar to *katouriso*, which means urination. In my broken Greek it sounded as if I wanted him to get on the scale so I could urinate on him. Maybe I was thinking that way because he had just come from his restaurant and smelled of grease and sweat.

Greeks do not like their wives to complain. One came with his wife to my office. She went on and on with many complaints. He sat there with a frown and finally said, in a disgusting voice, "Is there any area where you don't hurt?" She turned to him and said, "Yes, my ass." He raised his arm up and said, "I wish you were all ass."

A lady came to see me who had many complaints due to what she said was a brain tumor. I asked if a doctor had made that diagnosis, and she said, "No, but I can show you." She had a very large nose, and she spread her nostrils. Then she took a long hairpin from her hair that she straightened and pushed in one of her nostrils. Blood began to pour out and over my new desk. I said, "I am a cardiologist, and I don't take care of such problems." She said, "I know but someone told me you would listen to my story." I called an ear, nose, and throat specialist friend and said he had to see this patient immediately. Later that day I got a call from the specialist, and he said, "That patient you sent me has spilled blood all over my desk." We sent her to a psychiatrist.

Even as a heart specialist, I enjoyed making house calls for patients who were unable to come to my office. They were very grateful. Often they were elderly and poor. One had a small fish place in the old Charleston market. He lived with his wife in a small backroom off of his store. His wife was very sick from heart attacks. After I saw her, he would give me fish as payment.

A small service station operator twenty miles north of Charleston called me to see his wife. She had severe heart failure, and I had to visit her several times. He had just one gasoline pump and in his store several grocery items. It was obvious that he could just make ends meet so I never charged him. However, each time he gave me a jar of preserves his wife had made.

I often met my patients' families and had coffee or tea with them. In addition to their health, we discussed many of their other problems. I enjoyed this phase of my practice for the patients appreciated my services tremendously.

One such elderly patient lived alone, and he told me stories such as these.

Three men were killed in an automobile accident. St. Peter said to the first, "How many times did you cheat on your wife?" He said, "None." He gave him a Mercedes to drive in heaven. St. Peter asked the second one, "How many times did you cheat on your wife?" He said, "About seven times." He gave him a motorcycle. He asked the third one, "How many times did you cheat on your wife?" He said, "Many times," so St. Peter gave him a bicycle. One day the men on the motorcycle and bicycle saw the Mercedes parked. The driver inside was crying. "Why are you crying? You have a Mercedes," they said. "Yes, but I just saw my wife go by on roller skates."

Except for work, I had no hobbies. One day an old elementary school classmate called and wanted $35. He said he'd give me a set of golf clubs for it. I told him I had no use for his clubs since I never played the game. However, I met with him several times on one of the playgrounds for lessons. If I had persisted, I might have become a great golfer. Now I change my swing practically every time I play, but I certainly enjoy it. I was a great putter always, and my nickname to this day is Peter Putter. At age eighty, I had a hole in one. I mounted the ball in a shadow box with my golf scores and the signatures of the other three players. At home I took down a diploma to hang the shadow box. My wife came home and was upset. I explained that many can get diplomas but very few can get a hole in one.

I asked this fellow if he played golf. He said, "No, but I am not going to give it up."

This man came to the golf course with two pair of pants. Another man asked, "Why, two pair of pants?" Answer: "In case I get a hole in one."

Two men were playing behind two ladies who were playing very slow. One of the men went to ask the ladies to let them play through. He came running back and said, "I can't that's my wife and my mistress." The other fellow went and came running back and said, "It's a small world."

Building a private practice was not easy, and I had many obstacles to overcome *through the back door.* Association with my patients was well worth all the effort. The private practice of medicine before entering academic medicine made me understand and appreciate patients' problems.

CHAPTER 5

DIVISION OF CARDIOLOGY

Finally—No Superior

After ten years of private practice, the dean of the medical school called me to discuss cardiology. I had known Dr. Franklin Fetter from Philadelphia, where he was assistant superintendent of Philadelphia General Hospital. Internal medicine at the medical school was general medicine, and there were no subdivisions. To strengthen the department, he decided to divide it into divisions, and he wanted me to work full time at the medical school and develop the Cardiology Division. The chief of medicine was interested in cardiology, and I knew there would be a conflict. However, Dr. Fetter, again *through the back door*, said that I would be the director of cardiology and the chief of medicine would continue in his position. After a while, I became great friends with the chief of medicine because I was there not to usurp his position but to complement it. I took the position realizing my income would drop by at least 40 percent. As a part-time employee, I already spent a lot of time at the medical school. In addition, I enjoyed teaching and research. After consulting my family, I decided to accept the position. Interestingly, the IRS did not understand my drop in income, and twice a Mr. Marion Woodbury audited me. Marion later became vice president of finances at the medical school. I frequently reminded him of his audits.

Our division grew, and eventually we added several faculty members and cardiac fellowships. Many of the practicing cardiologists in our state (and other states) had their training at our school. I published over 200 articles, wrote eighteen chapters in textbooks, and was the sole author of the textbook *Clinical Cardiology: A Bedside Approach* which is now in its fourth edition. This book is now sold all over the world. *Cardiology Pearls,* a book that I wrote with Dr. Blase Carabello, is now in its second edition.

I received many awards for teaching. Three times I was given the student American Medical Association Golden Apple Award. The honor that I cherish most is the National Gifted Teacher Award from the American College of Cardiology. I received the Order of the Palmetto, the highest State of South Carolina award, from Republican Governor David Beasley, and the Order of the Silver Crescent from Democratic Governor Jim Hodges. I am one of a few selected as an honorary member of the American Academy of Family Physicians. The American Heart Association awarded me a Lifetime Achievement Award. I also received an honorary degree of doctor of letters from the College of Charleston and an honorary degree of doctor of science from the Citadel. The Citadel award was indeed *through the back door* since they had turned me down for a college scholarship.

On October 11, 1996, the cardiovascular research building was dedicated in my name. On June 1, 2008, Dr. Peter C. Gazes Endowed Chair in Clinical Cardiology was established at the Medical University of South Carolina. In addition to serving as the Distinguished Clinical University Professor of Cardiology at the Medical University, I served on many national medical committees and received numerous awards. The Orthodox Christian Church appointed me an archon, which is one of the highest awards a layperson can receive in this church. In 2003, I was selected and listed in the book *Profiles in Cardiology,* a collection of profiles featuring individuals who have made significant contributions to the study of cardiovascular disease. I have lectured in many countries.

One time after I gave a talk, an elderly doctor came up to me and said, "That was the worst talk I ever heard." I was despondent, but a young doctor came up and said, "Don't listen to him. He is senile and just repeats what other people say."

After a talk, I gave my honorarium back to the moderator. He said, "Thank you. We will use it to get a better speaker next time."

I've been visiting Marion and Florence, South Carolina, for over thirty years, seeing patients and lecturing. Once in Marion, I had time to play golf with Dr. Glen Askins. Just before finishing, it began sleeting, and I heard a bell tinkling. I asked Dr. Askins, "Why would an ice cream man be out on a day like this?" He laughed and said, "That is a cow bell." Another time, a doctor and I went to Marion for a golf game and a medical meeting. We were only allowed to use a car from the medical university car pool. At 10:00 that night, we headed home. We had a flat tire. It took several minutes to find the spare, which was in our station wagon's side panel. The road we were on was narrow and with ditches on both sides. It was very dark. Therefore, we kept the car lights on. After changing the tire, the car would not start. The battery was dead. Fortunately, a car came, and a man stepped out to help us. Fearing a robbery, one of us stood behind the car with a lug wrench. It turned out the man was a good Samaritan, and he had jumper cables to restart our car.

On the way again we thought the gas gauge registered a full tank. It was defective, and the car stopped. Out of gasoline! We could see lights about a mile ahead, so I walked toward them and found a nightclub. It was Saturday, and there was much eating, drinking, and dancing. One woman grabbed me and wanted to dance.

I had seen a closed gasoline station nearby. I asked at the nightclub for the station owner's telephone number. I called him. He was upset because it was 1:00 A.M., and I had awakened him. At first refused, he to open his station but asked who I was. When I told him, his attitude changed. He said, "Oh, Dr. Gazes—you treated my wife at the medical university. I'll be right over." Again, a *through the back door* experience.

My brother Pat often would go with me on my lecturing trips. I would always have a box of cheese crackers that he ate on the way. One day he said, "You know I have heard you speak so often, I think I could give your talk."

A physician's chauffer, John, said on the way to a meeting. "I have heard you so often, let me give your talk tonight." Since he had not been seen previously by that night's audience, the physician allowed his chauffer to do so while he sat in the back of the room. After the chauffer's talk, someone asked a question. John cleverly said, "My chauffer in the back of the room will answer that."

We were coming back from Florence one night and listening to stories on tape by the comedian Jackie Mason. After driving many miles, we realized we were near Savannah. We had missed our exit. Since we were low on gasoline, we stopped at a station. My brother Pat pumped the gas, and I went to pay. Not realizing I had come in, someone closed the door and turned out the lights. At that moment, a patrol car drove up, and the patrolman thought that Pat and I were robbing the station. I found a light switch and told the owner, who was in the back, what happened. After much explaining, we were allowed to proceed. Talking of policemen...

A Greek priest and a rabbi were in a wreck. The rabbi said, "You know we are friends, and I have some good wine. Let's have a drink until the policeman comes." He poured two glasses and the Greek priest drank his. He asked the rabbi, "You haven't touched yours." He said, "Yes, I am waiting on the policeman."

The Division of Cardiology at the Medical University of Charleston became one of the most advanced and esteemed heart programs in the southeast. After twenty-five years as its leader, I stepped down to devote my time to teaching and research. The division was taken over by Dr. Jim Spann, who served as head for ten years. He turned it over to Dr. Michael Assey. I had watched Michael advance through his internship, residency, fellowship, attending physician, and the head of cardiology. He was a wonderful person and clinician. He died suddenly from viral myocarditis (infection of the muscle of the heart).

Since my interest has been in coronary heart disease, I would like to clarify the meaning of *heart attack* and give some additional information about coronary heart disease.

The heart is a muscle that pumps oxygen-rich blood throughout the body. The coronary arteries (three major vessels with many branches) lie on the surface of the heart, and their branches carry nutrients straight to the heart muscle.

If these arteries stay healthy and unclogged, the heart usually gets all the oxygen it needs. Plaque is a bulge in a coronary artery that is attributable to atherosclerosis. Atherosclerosis is composed of several types of cells, smooth muscle, calcium, fatlike deposits and inflammatory mediators. The plaque develops along the vessel wall and narrows its opening, which interferes with blood flow to the heart muscle (the same as squeezing a garden hose and blocking the flow of water). As a result, the coronary arteries may become narrow with partial blockage and produce lower jaw, neck, arm, or chest pain referred to as stable or unstable angina. The discomfort is usually dull, heavy, pressurelike or squeezing but not often sharp. In unstable angina, usually a plaque ruptures and a clot forms, further reducing the coronary artery opening but does not produce total closure. Stable angina is not associated with plaque rupture. It is angina that has not changed in character, intensity, or frequency over a period of several months or more, and it usually occurs with exertion. Unstable angina is the initial onset of frequent angina or a sudden increase in stable angina or angina at rest.

When a major coronary artery branch is totally or partially blocked, many cardiac cells die and damage the heart muscle, and enzymes go up significantly;

this is a so-called heart attack (myocardial infarction). The term acute coronary syndrome (ACS), often mentioned on television refers to unstable angina and the heart attack. Patients with a heart attack have prolonged symptoms for at least twenty minutes. Unless there are complications, the physical examination may reveal no significant finding. The electrocardiogram (ECG) will have positive findings in 60 percent of cases, atypical findings in 30 percent, and in 10 percent the tracing can be normal. I have heard stories of someone going to a doctor with chest pain and being told not to worry because their ECG was normal. Later that day a heart attack occurred. The echocardiogram and coronary imaging studies (CAT scan, calcium score, and MRI) are helpful in some cases to confirm the diagnosis and to assess the degree of cardiac damage. All heart attacks today are monitored in coronary care units. Cardiac arrest can occur as an ineffective beat called ventricular fibrillation. Now such patients can be shocked and normal rhythm restored. This alone has reduced mortality considerably.

When coronary care units first opened, I had two patients with heart attacks being monitored by electrocardiogram. The old patient told the new patient that he will be wired and his electrocardiogram will be shown on the TV screen and with each heart beat there will be a beeping sound. He said if that beeping stops, you better start saying, "Beep, beep, otherwise they will come in and beat the hell out of you."

As mentioned above, usually with a heart attack, a plaque in the coronary artery ruptures and forms a clot that completely closes the opening of the vessel. Medications can be given to dissolve the clot and help restore blood flow. Patients should be advised that if they have a discomfort in the chest that radiates to the neck, lower jaw, left arm, or both arms, they should chew a plain five-grain aspirin (unless they are allergic) and go to an emergency department immediately. I think it is important to note that the discomfort may occur only in one area. It may be only in the chest, only in the jaw, only in the neck or throat, or only in the left arm, or even only in the right arm. At least 365,000 women in the United States die yearly of coronary artery disease. Most of the clinical trials included only males. As a result, females have been less aware of the importance of the usual symptoms of a heart attack. In addition, females have other symptoms, such as a sudden increase in weakness, shortness of breath, extreme fatigue, nausea, upper abdominal pain, mid-upper back pain, or indigestion. Premonitory symptoms serve as a warning several days before an attack may be fatigue, dyspnea (shortness of breath), and sleep disturbance. These heart attacks occur after menopause usually ten years later than in males.

Geographic age of women: From fifteen to twenty-five years of age she is like Africa—half virgin, half explored. From age twenty-five to thirty-five, she is like Asia—hot, torrid, and mysterious. From thirty-five to forty-five she is like America— streamlined, efficient, and cooperative. From forty-five to fifty-five years she is like Europe—devastated but still good. After fifty-five years she is like Australia— everyone knows where it is, but nobody goes there.

It is wise to carry a plain aspirin (5 grains 325 mg), with you, and if symptoms typical or atypical (as noted in females) occur anywhere above your waist that has not been previously diagnosed, chew the aspirin and seek help. If the attack turns out not to be due to cardiac problems, you have done no harm. However, in case of a heart attack, the aspirin may partially dissolve the clot and allow some blood flow through the coronary vessel and prevent some damage to the heart. Further resolution of the clot may be accomplished by fibrinolytic agents (so-called clot busters). Since fibrinolytic agents can cause hemorrhage or have several undesirable effects, often today a patient is taken directly to the cardiac catheterization labora-tory without giving such agents. In this lab, a slender tube (a catheter) is inserted through a leg artery and guided into the heart and a contrast agent is injected into the coronary arteries so they can be visualized. The catheter has a balloon at its tip that is inflated into the obstructed opening, compress-ing the plaque against the artery wall. This is called angioplasty. Most often today the catheter also contains a stent (a stainless steel mesh or coil) that is inserted after the angioplasty and serves as a scaffold to keep the vessel open. There is still an ongoing debate as to which stent is the best. Newer stents are constantly being developed. In some instances the obstruction may not be suitable for stents and may require coronary bypass surgery. Since a high percentage of patients have small asymptomatic coronary plaques that may rupture, methods are being developed to detect these. Persons who have risk factors such as high blood pressure (hypertension), high lipid levels (cholesterol and triglycerides), sedentary lifestyle, obesity, diabetes, smoking, and have a family history of coronary disease should be aware that they are at risk to have a heart attack. Small plaques will not cause changes in a stress test. Calcium score (electron beam computed tomography-EBCT), multislice rapid CT scanner, MRI (magnetic resonance imaging), and nuclear methods may be useful noninvasive imaging methods to detect the plaques in those at risk. If a patient has a negative calcium score, they have less than 0.1 percent per year (up to ten years) of having a heart attack. The atherosclerotic plaque is a part of a spectrum of diseases (coronary artery disease, carotid disease, and peripheral vascular disease) that can be modified by controlling blood pressure and diabetes, eating fewer high-cholesterol and high-fat foods, refraining from smoking, getting regular exercise (walking three miles per day is excellent), and maintaining normal body weight. Controlling these risk factors can prevent plaque formation and cause some regression in the already formed atherosclerotic plaque, which reduces the chances of angina or a heart attack.

Inside the nucleus of every cell there are pairs of chromosomes that contain thousands of genes. Each gene is made up of segments of DNA that hold the recipe for making specific proteins. The cause of coronary artery disease is unknown. It is polygenetic (many genes) Many of these genes that contribute to coronary artery disease have not been identified. However, these genes will interact with environmental influences such as risk factors for coronary artery disease.

The way you can tell the sex of a chromosome is by pulling down it's genes.

In addition to hospitalized patients, I saw many in the outpatient department. One of my great interests was to take a detailed history, especially if patients were over eighty-years- old. I wanted to know about their childhood activities, namely, if they exercised, their dietary habits, and any other factors that might have influenced their health. I had one eighty-five-year-old gentleman as a patient, and while interrogating him he said, "You know, doctor, I have a bowel movement every morning at eight o'clock." I replied, "For your age that is great." Then he confided, "Yes, but I don't get up until nine o'clock." Another person told me he lived long because he walked slowly, sat loosely, and when he had any worries, he would fall asleep. I asked a little old lady who was about eighty-six-years-old if she had ever smoked or drank, and she said, "No." I asked, "Were you ever bedridden?" She said in a low voice, "Yes, but don't put that in my record."

In nursing homes, we give elderly males Viagra, so they will not fall out of bed.

I was in the examining room, and I told the nurse, Mary Washington, that I was going to wash my hands. She said, "There is a basin in this room, why are you going elsewhere to wash your hands." I immediately answered, "Do you want me to pee in the basin?" She didn't realize when a man states that he wants to wash his hands, he intends to go to the bathroom. Likewise, when a lady says she is going to powder her nose, she goes to the restroom.

It is most rewarding when you can do something for your patient. A twelve-year-old boy was referred to me because he had a congenital heart

defect (meaning present at birth). He had a very small opening in the parti-
tion between two lower chambers of the heart. His greatest problem would
be an infection that could cause endocarditis (infection on the sides of the
opening). His teeth were very carious (rotten), and prone to infection and
endocarditis. They could not afford a dentist. I told his mother that I would
not charge for my services, and to use the money to see a dentist and then
report back to me. I told my wife this story. Forty years later the lady came
up to me with her son and asked if I remembered him? He was now a large,
handsome man. After his mother repeated the story, my wife, who was sitting
next to me, smiled.

Another rewarding experience was that of a lady who died. For several
months, her son came to my office by bicycle. I asked my secretary what
his problem was. He came monthly to pay $2.00 on his late mother's bill.
I canceled it. Such are the rewards we get in medicine.

As an academician, I could practice medicine, teach, and be involved in
research. Developing a strong division of cardiology was very difficult. Again,
I had to overcome many obstacles *through the back door*.

CHAPTER 6
MEDICAL STUDENTS
Teaching Is Rewarding

One of the greatest rewards in academic medicine is teaching. A career in medicine was very popular until several years ago when the application pool dropped. Now it is rising again. Brighter students are being attracted. One can now enter the medical profession as a family physician, teacher, specialist, or researcher. Students have two years of basic science followed by two clinical years. There are many variations. Some schools introduce patient care within basic sciences. Today's physician is so much better trained and equipped than when I was a student. In the last fifty years, cardiology has become a specialty with unbelievable advances. Pacemakers, coronary bypass surgery, heart transplants, and cardiac drugs—these are just a few of the many advances. Students rotate through the various disciplines, and they eventually sort out what they like best. Besides hospital work, much of their training is in clinics. We now have simulators that can produce heart sounds and murmurs just as those heard in humans. These are available and can be referred to at any time. As professors, our job is to keep abreast of new developments and explain to the students that a good history and physical examination are still essential. These things cannot be replaced by instrumentation.

Echocardiography, heart catheterization, and other studies should be done when there is a definite indication. The cost of medicine rises when physicians order these tests indiscriminately. It is not necessary to repeat these studies unless there is a change in the history and physical examination. The demands are many today, but we teach our students that the greatest responsibility is the patient. They should be taught to explain the patient's condition in a simple manner that can clearly be understood. This was brought to my attention several years ago by a college graduate, after I had explained in detail her father's heart attack and mentioned how the coronary arteries were obstructed. She looked at me and said, "I am grateful that it was not his heart, and it was just his arteries." I had spent much time on the obstructed vessel but failed to emphasize that this obstruction caused a reduced blood supply with resultant damage to the muscle of the heart. So even to the brightest, we should take time and ensure that they understand what is going on.

I have many interesting stories growing out of my association with students. One day I lectured to a class that study of the heart must be done in conjunction with study of the lungs, the kidneys, and the brain. I said they must be very observant.

A container of a patient's urine was sitting on my desk, and I put my finger in it and then licked the finger. I said that laboratory tests were important but physically examining different specimens of patients were, too. I had each of the students come forward, insert an index finger in the urine, and lick it. Afterward I said, "I doubt that many of you will be good doctors because you didn't observe very well." I had placed my index finger in the urine, but I licked my middle finger.

A student wrote on his exam that only God knows the answer to one of my questions. I sent the exam back with "You-zero; God-100." Another time, I gave students a case with many findings and asked what they would do for the patient. One of my students said, "I would call Dr. Gazes in for consultation." I gave him a perfect grade.

One time I lectured for two hours. After the first hour, I allowed the students to stand for a rest. A student near me said, "Thanks, Dr. Gazes—my buttocks fell asleep." I answered, "I know. I heard it snore twice."

In the 1970s and 1980s, there were many "maverick" students. They did not dress well and were not well groomed. On one of my rounds, I saw a student with long hair and a beard that covered practically all of his face. I told him he looked like an armpit with teeth. The students so harassed him that the next day he came back clean shaven.

I often get telephone calls, letters, or visits from former students. They remind me of many comments I made. Dr. Tom Rowland, an obstetrician and gynecologist, who is on our Medical University of Charleston's Board of Trustees and a past chairman, often tells this story. After graduation he came by my office and said, "Dr. Gazes, I thank you for your teaching, and if I ever have chest pain, I will come see you." He says I answered, "Son, by the time you have chest pain, you will not be able to afford me." Once, at a large medical university affair, I had to introduce him and was given two minutes to do so. I said, "After reviewing Dr. Rowland's curriculum vitae, I think I need only one minute."

At Myrtle Beach, South Carolina, I met a former student who graduated over twenty years ago and now practices psychiatry in Washington, DC. He remembered that while a student, just after marriage, he wanted to impress his wife by cooking the Thanksgiving turkey. I gave him the following recipe: Season the turkey with salt, pepper, and garlic salt. Squeeze lemon all over the skin, outside, and inside. Place the turkey in a pan with about two inches of water. Chop celery, carrots, onions, and bell pepper into the water, along with the turkey's neck and stomach. Cook it twenty minutes per pound. The water and ingredients will make the gravy. He said that every year since then he baked his turkey the same way.

There was a man that lived near my father's grocery store who was a hypochondriac. Our parrot bit him, and several of his friends asked me, as a medical student, to make up a disease. I stared at him and told him his skin was green, and he probably had parrot sickness (psittacosis). As a teacher, I told my students to bring a patient with congestive heart failure to the class, so that I could demonstrate the findings. The patient turned out to be the one whom I had told, years before, that he had parrot's disease. When I came into the class, he jumped up and ran down the hall. He was afraid I would again make an unusual diagnosis.

At one time, I was working with a Ballistocardiogram. With each heartbeat, blood is ejected into the aorta, and your body actually moves. This movement can be detected by a Ballistocardiogram. I thought that this would be a good way to measure heart strength noninvasively. A hammock that weighed about two pounds was suspended with strong wires to a very large screw in the ceiling. The patient would lie on the hammock, which coupled to his body; with each heartbeat, the hammock would move. This movement was recorded by a magnet and an electric coil. To test this, I selected various students. It worked well until I choose a 200-pound student for study. When this student lay on the hammock, the screw came out of the ceiling, along with a lot of plaster, which covered him where he lay on the floor. The crash was heard all over the hospital. Fortunately, the student was not hurt.

Monthly, I had a journal club meeting with students. We usually went to a quiet bar and discussed medical articles over a beer. At one meeting, a man came and sat at our table. He began drinking our beer. I realized that he was an elementary school classmate whom I had not seen for many years. His nickname was Mink. The students were surprised that I knew such a character. Mink often liked to watch wrestling on television. And that reminds me of an Olympic story:

An American and Russian were in the finals of a wrestling match for a gold medial. The coach told the American, "Don't let him get you in the twister hold because nobody has been able to break it. At the start of the match, however, the Russian got him in the twister. The coach lowered his head because he knew the gold medal was lost. He heard the roar of the crowd and looked up, and they were holding up the American's arm as the winner. Afterward, his wrestler said the Russian was very fast and had him in the twister before he got started. "All I could see were arms, legs, and a pair of testicles, so I bit them." The coach said, "How did that get you loose?" He answered, "They were my own."

Today, medical students represent the profession very well. The patients also see the difference. Our students are well groomed and dressed, kind, compassionate, and knowledgeable.

I've lectured to nurses, physician assistants, and others. Each morning I read ECGs with students. Often I told them I love the ECG because it sent my three daughters through college and my wife through Neiman Marcus. If my wife doesn't go to Neiman Marcus once a year, they send her a get-well card. In fact, I want to be cremated and have my ashes thrown over Neiman Marcus because I know my wife will visit me there often.

These are some Gazesisms I often quoted to students.

Death — I don't care if I die; I just don't want to be there when it happens. I want my patients to live longer and die younger.

Health — If I had known that I would live this long, I would have taken better care of myself.

Diet — Reach for your mate rather than your plate. Skim whiskey for fat men and bourbon suppositories for patients with duodenal ulcers. Candy — a moment on your lips and forever on your hips.

Definitions – The blood going away from the heart is arterial and the blood returning to the heart is venereal.

Auscultation (listening to the heart) – Listen long; listen wrong.

Overheard – Medical student saying, "Could finish medical school in two years if it wasn't for the elevators."

Example – No one is worthless for they can always be used as a bad example.

Cancer – Don't throw your cigarette butts on the floor—our cockroaches are getting cancer.

Hemorrhoid treatment: Preparation H and vodka—a pile driver cocktail. *Innuendo* is the Italian trade name for Preparation H.

Credit cards – A man lost a card. Friend: "Did you report it?" Man: "Why should I? The person who found it is spending less than my wife."

Golf – A good walk ruined.

Advice – Be quick to listen but slow to respond.

Greeks – Why do Greeks look young? Thank the Lord for Grecian formula and Preparation H.

Double blind study – Two surgeons reading an electrocardiogram.

My philosophy – Persistence and determination alone are omnipotent.

Reputation is what you think you are, but character is what you really are.

I'd rather be miserable and alive than happy and dead.

Advertisement – A laxative that works while you sleep.

Laughter is internal jogging.

Life is short—that's why I always eat my dessert first and never buy green bananas.

Patient on seafood diet—he eats all he can see.

Every time I see this guy, I wish that birth control were retroactive.

Today's life – Too many parents tie up their dogs and let their children run loose.

Miniskirts are like the cost of living. Neither can go much higher.

Honeymoon – Take your wife to Viagra Falls.

For me today, getting some action means my prune juice is working.

I need glasses to find my glasses.

Getting even: I want to live long enough to be a problem to my children.

Here are a few suggestions that may help doctors regain respect and image:

Patients should be your major concern. They are worried and concerned, and they need your sympathy and a good explanation of their problem. As Hippocrates said, "Without love for his fellow man, no man can love medicine."

Families are frightened, and they need to be informed of the situation.

Be kind to service workers, e.g., your secretary, the elevator operator, etc.

Welcome a second opinion; recognize your limitations.

Do not make medicine big business. Hippocrates had many aphorisms, e.g., "Setting a fee should be secondary to caring for and reassuring the patient." "Discussing fees may increase the patient's anxiety and be harmful to him."

Keep abreast of changes. Constantly be eager to learn because a physician has a great opportunity, as he grows older, to continue developing and practicing his art. This may not be the case in other professions. Remember your education has just begun.

Hippocrates' first aphorism by itself is almost a sufficient moral precept for the practice of medicine, and I quote, "Life is short, whereas the demands of the medical profession are unending, the crisis is urgent, experiment dangerous, and decision difficult. But the physician must not only do what is necessary, he must also get the patient, the attendants, and the external factors to work together to the same end."

Being a part of a student's career is very satisfying. I have followed the careers of many and saw them develop into wonderful physicians. It is very rewarding to receive calls, letters, and visits from them. Very often I tell students they must be scientific to the disease, and humane to the patient. If they do this, they will overcome any obstacle *through the back door*.

CHAPTER 7
MY HEALTH

Whistle While You Work

I have been very fortunate to have good health. Now at age eighty-eight, three times a week I walk twenty-five minutes on the treadmill, perform twenty-five minutes on the rowing machine, and ten minutes of calisthenics. The other days, I play golf. I practice what I preach because I emphasize maintaining body weight with regular exercise, not smoking, controlling blood pressure, and adhering to good nutrition. During the past two decades, there has been overwhelming evidence that high serum cholesterol is linked to coronary heart disease (angina and heart attack). However, we should realize that there are many other aspects of cholesterol that are very important. Cholesterol and triglycerides (true fats) do not circulate in the blood as such, but together with proteins form the lipoproteins that circulate in the blood. There are three important major types of lipoproteins that have different amounts of cholesterol, triglycerides, and protein. Low-density lipoprotein (LDL) is the bad actor because it contains predominantly cholesterol and less triglycerides and protein. Very low-density lipoprotein (VLDL) contains mostly triglycerides, and high-density lipoprotein (HDL), the good actor, has mostly protein. Therefore, our aim should be to have a decrease in LDL and VLDL, and an increase in HDL. Lipoprotein LP(a), which has a larger particle attached to LDL, is often measured for it may also be associated with coronary heart disease.

After fasting for twelve hours, blood levels can be measured for cholesterol, triglycerides, LDL, VLDL, and HDL. The total cholesterol level measured is extracted from the lipoproteins. Ideal blood levels for each are as follows: cholesterol less than 200 mg, triglycerides less than 150 mg, HDL 60 mg or more, LDL 100 mg or less, and VLDL less than 30 mg. My levels are normal except for a borderline HDL. Patients with coronary artery disease should strive to get LDL down to 60-80 mg. Unfortunately, many people who develop coronary heart disease have normal LDL, VLDL, and HDL levels. Research has shown that the lipoproteins have subclasses that play an important part in heart health. For example, one may have a LDL level below 100 mg, yet that is not good because in its subclass LDL has small bad particles rather than good particles. Likewise, HDL and VLDL have subclasses with large particles that are bad for VLDL and good for HDL, even though the total levels of these may be normal. At present, there are few laboratories that measure the subclass levels.

A metabolic syndrome was recognized in a number of patients. This syndrome has three or more of these components: abdominal obesity, insulin resistance with or without diabetes, hypertension, hypertriglyceridemia, low HDL, and an increase in the bad small particles of LDL. Abdominal visceral obesity has become important as body mass index (BMI). BMI is calculated as weight/height (Kg/m^2). Measurements of 25-29 indicate overweight and above 30, obesity. Men's waist $\geq$ 40 inches and women's waist of $\geq$ 35 inches and waist/hip ratio in men >.9 and female > .85 are defined by the American Heart Association and the Heart, Lung and Blood Institute as abdominal obesity. The BMI may be normal, and yet the patient has an increase in abdominal obesity. Fortunately all my measurements are normal.

Today, the management of lipid disorders encourages diet and early use of drugs. Many weight reduction diets have been advocated, such as the low fat, high fat, low carb, high carb, high protein, low protein, and many others. Regardless of the type of diet, calories have to be counted.

A patient went to a doctor who prescribed several diets, but the patient still did not lose weight. Finally, the doctor said, "We will wire your mouth." The patient said, "Then how will I eat?" The doctor said, "You will feed yourself through the rectum." He returned in three months, and the doctor said, "You look great, and you have lost several pounds. But why are you wiggling and twisting?" The patient said, "I am chewing gum."

A man went to a restaurant and ordered dinner. After he finished the manager asked, "How did you like the meal?" He said, "Wonderful, but you gave me only two slices of bread." The manager asked, "Will you return tomorrow?" The next day he returned, and the manager told the waitress to get a whole loaf of bread. Afterward he asked again, "Did you like the meal?" The man said, "Yes, but you didn't give me enough bread." Again, he was asked if he would return. The next day he came back, and the manager told the waitress to get a two-foot long loaf of bread and cut it in half. Afterward, the manager said, "Did you like the meal today?" The man said, "Yes, but why did you go back to two slices of bread?"

In addition to counting calories, the kind of food eaten is very important. Some choices may not stimulate the brain's appetite center. Most processed, refined carbohydrates (white carbs) are digested quickly and produce a sudden rise of sugar in your blood. The spike in blood sugar signals the pancreas to release insulin, which drives sugar into cells and promotes fat storage. Blood sugar rapidly falls. The brain is dependent on glucose and responds by stimulating the appetite center, and further intake of white carbs that elevate blood sugar. The glycemic index rates foods as to how they affect your blood sugar level. The refined white carbs (white rice, white potatoes, white flour) raise the blood sugar quickly (high glycemic index), compared to foods that are digested slowly. The blood sugar level remains steady with the right carbs with a low glycemic index such as whole grains, nonstarchy vegetables, fruits, and beans that are digested slowly. Starchy vegetables are potatoes, corn, and rutabagas.

Obesity is definitely a cardiac risk factor and therefore calories have to be counted. Thirty percent of the calories should be fat calories. A simple calculation can be made as follows. For a patient allowed 1,000 calories daily: 30 percent of 1,000 is 300 calories from fats. Read food labels to get nutrition facts to find out what you are eating. To calculate the percentage of fat per serving, take the number of fat calories and divide by the total number of calories per serving to get the percentage, which should not be over 30 percent. Each gram of fat has 9 calories; therefore, 9 divided into 300 (30 percent fat calories in a 1,000 calorie diet) gives approximately 33 grams. The patient can consume on a 1,000 calorie diet, 33 grams of fat. However, most important is the type of fat. The National Cholesterol Education Program (NCEP) Panel III recommends intake of saturated fats (red meats, whole dairy products) to less then 7 percent of the total daily caloric intake, polyunsaturated fats (as corn, safflower, and soybean oils) up to 10 percent, and monounsaturated fats (canola, olive oil, and peanut oil) up to 20 percent. Exercise along with diet is essential for weight loss. To lose one pound you have to expend about 3,500 calories. If you briskly walk three miles daily, you will burn 300 calories.

Therefore, in ten to twelve days without change of diet you'd lose one pound. A saying I like is At night reach for your mate rather than your plate.

I asked an obese lady, "What was your lowest body weight?" She answered, "Seven pounds, eight ounces."

One day a lady saw me in the hallway and said, "Look doctor, I have lost ten pounds. Not thinking, I said, "Turn around, and you will find it."

Monounsaturated fats are the best for they can increase HDL. Saturated fats have high cholesterol content and are high risk for coronary heart disease. Generally, saturated fats are solid, but some may be liquid such as palm and coconut oils. When shopping, learn to read labels because they list the content and type of fats. In addition, avoid foods labeled as hydrogenated for this means that many of the polyunsaturated oils have been transformed into solid saturated fats (trans-fatty acids). Trans-fatty acids are found when liquid vegetable oils are partially hydrogenated to form margarine and shortenings. Hydrogenation makes food last longer and look better. For example, oil would float above when old-time peanut butter sat on the shelf. This looked bad and could become rancid. Crackers would often grow soft if they were out of the box too long. Hydrogenation made peanut butter solid and kept crackers crispy. These trans-fats have the same detrimental effects as saturated fats that increase cholesterol and lower HDL. Eating fish has become popular for it has the polyunsaturated omega-3 fatty acids, which can reduce triglycerides, cardiovascular events, and sudden cardiac arrest. Fish oil capsule supplements are recommended primarily for very high triglyceride levels. It is best to get omega-3 by eating at least two to three fish meals per week. Most effective are the darker fatty fishes such as salmon. The white fishes are good, but in large amounts some of them (namely, swordfish and shark) may increase the intake of mercury, and that in turn can cause heart damage. Shellfish are high in cholesterol but also have significant omega-3 fatty acids and therefore can be eaten once a week. A good saying that I have used for years is If it can swim or fly, eat it.

Our family diet (the Mediterranean type) was vastly different than it is today. The Mediterranean diet emphasizes whole grains, fish, olive oil, garlic, a moderate amount of wine, and healthy nutrients such as omega-3 fatty acids. Olive oil was the only oil used. If I ever become president of the Medical University, I will insist that all procedures be done with olive oil. Our main family meal would be soup, chicken or fish, very little red meat, and lots of fruits and vegetables.

Speaking about diet...

This man had the furniture syndrome; his chest fell into his drawers.

A man told a psychiatrist his brother thought he was a chicken. The psychiatrist said "Well, bring him to me, and I will cure him." The man said, "No, you can't do that. Our family needs the eggs."

My family did not smoke or drink excessive alcohol. In fact, I never have taken a puff on a cigarette. I drank my first alcohol at my medical school graduation party.

There is a cigarette anonymous club. A man called the club office and said he craved a cigarette. He was told not to smoke but to come on over. He went there, and the two got drunk together.

O'Reilly was dying and asked O'Malley to sprinkle a pint of whiskey over his grave. O'Malley answered, "I'll do it, provided you let it pass through my kidneys first."

In simple terms, I tell my patients they should eat three fish meals a week (at least one should be salmon), skinless chicken three times a week, and red meat only once a week. The diet should include five or more servings per day of fruits and vegetables, the right carbohydrates, and whole-wheat pastas and breads. The oil should be olive or canola, and if a glass of red wine is added, you will have the Mediterranean diet. Omega-3 fortified eggs can be eaten but not more than one daily.

There was an Indian who had a fabulous memory. A doctor interested in memory research went to the reservation and asked the Indian, "What did you have for breakfast twenty years ago?" He said, "Eggs." Ten years later the doctor returned to the reservation to see if the Indian still had a good memory. The Indian was then ninety years old. He was seated in a chair when the doctor raised an arm and said, "How." The Indian said, "Scrambled."

Speaking of memory...

I was at a nursing home one day, and this elderly lady kept looking at me. I assumed she was an old patient and asked her, "Do you know who I am?" She stated, "No, but if you go to the nursing station, they will tell you."

An elderly couple was looking at television, and the husband told his wife, "I am going to the kitchen, do you want anything?" She said, "Yes—ice cream. But write it down or you will forget it." He said, "Do you want anything else?" She said, "Yes— chocolate syrup on the ice cream. But write it down or you will forget." He said, "No, I won't." Thirty minutes later he came back with scrambled eggs. She said, "I knew you would forget. Where's the bacon?"

Red wine and grape juice affect vascular lesions and may increase HDL. A twelve-ounce bottle of beer, a four-ounce glass of red wine, or a one-and-one-half-ounce shot of eighty-proof whiskey contain the same amount of alcohol (one-half ounce). Each is considered a *drink equivalent*. One to two drinks daily are recommended. National guidelines recommend caution, since clinical care requires consideration of the myriad health effects of alcohol and an individual's susceptibility to it.

In college, I took a date to dinner, and I asked if she preferred red or white wine. She said, "It doesn't matter. I'm color blind."

Drinking coffee may increase excretion of calcium, which could increase the risk of high blood pressure. It appears that unfiltered coffee (Turkish, boiled, French press, and espresso) raises cholesterol. One study suggested coffee increases levels of homocysteine, which is an amino acid product that may increase the risk of heart attacks. Its blood level can be measured. However, a clear association of homocysteine with coronary artery disease has not been shown. Decaf does not raise this level. Tea (especially green and black), even though it may contain caffeine, has folic acid, which may protect against homocysteine. It also contains antioxidants. Oxidative (combine with oxygen) reactions produce free radicals that damage cells. Antioxidants are chemicals that block oxidation. They also prevent oxidation of the bad actor LDL so it will not get into the coronary vessels and aid in plaque production. Many foods are rich in antioxidants, namely, berries.

A study reported in the *Circulation* journal May 2, 2006, shows that consumption of six or more cups of coffee per day does not increase coronary heart disease. Decaffeinated coffee, tea, and caffeine intake were also unrelated to coronary heart disease risk. Short-term consumption provides similar results as long term use, and were not significantly associated with lipid levels.

Dark chocolate has high cocoa content and increased flavonoids, which are chemical compounds also found in many other foods, especially fruits and vegetables, and have potent antioxidant properties. Flavonoid – rich chocolate also improves coronary vascular function and decreases platelet adhesion, which can form clots. The color of the chocolate and the percent of cocoa do not give a measure of flavonoids. One to two ounces per day is recommended. Avoid excessive amounts because chocolate also contains sugar and fat.

Many types of diets have been touted. The Ornish diet is very low in fat. It reduces total fat to 10 percent of calories. This diet excludes all oils and animal products, and should be used only by those who have extreme lipid abnormalities. Close supervision by a physician is required when on this diet.

"This lady's husband was losing interest in her, and a friend said, "Tonight, get nude, and wrap yourself in Saran Wrap. Greet him this way at the door." She did, and when he saw her, he said, "Not leftovers again."

My interest in diet led to my being invited by many organizations as a luncheon or dinner speaker. The Columbia Dietetic Association invited me to speak at their annual banquet in Columbia, South Carolina. When I arrived, no one noticed me. Finally, I approached one of the ladies and said I was their speaker. Frantically, she raised her arms and ran. After several minutes, she returned with the president of the organization. The Columbia Newspaper had published the wrong picture of me. The picture was of a bald, 250-pound man with large, black-rimmed glasses. My wife received many letters from friends asking, "What have you done to poor Pete?" Another time, the wives club at the Charleston U.S. Air Force Base invited me to speak at their luncheon. They were honoring some wives who were leaving because their husbands had been transferred. During a wine reception, some spoke about their friends and cried. I was supposed to talk at noon but it was 3:00 P.M. before I was introduced. Lunch was even later. By the time it was served, we should have had dinner.

This hunter went out to kill a grizzly bear. He did not see any, so he propped his rifle against a tree and went to wash his face in a nearby pond. When he came back, a large grizzly bear was waiting for him. The hunter got on his knees and prayed, "Dear God, please make this grizzly bear be a Christian." The bear raised his arms up and stated, "Thank you, God, for allowing me to partake of this wonderful meal."

Diet is very important, and often this is combined with antilipid agents for best results. The statin drugs reduce LDL significantly; triglycerides less so but minimally raise HDL. Atorvastatin (Lipitor), simvastatin (Zocor), pravastatin (Pravachol), fluvastatin (Lescol), lovastatin (Mevacor), and rosuvastatin (Crestor) are all effective but vary in strength and have some small differences. They have other effects besides those on lipids. They improve vessel wall function, and reduce clots and inflammation, which often occur at the site of blockage in the coronary vessel. C-reactive protein blood level, which is a marker for inflammation, can be reduced by statin drugs. Statin drugs are being used today even in patients with normal lipids, in view of their direct effects on coronary vessels.

The best all around lipid-modifying agent is niacin because it not only reduces cholesterol, total LDL and its bad small particles, and triglycerides, but also significantly increases HDL. For many years, there was not a suitable preparation available with few side effects. Extended-release niacin (Niaspan) is now available and has been shown to be very effective, and has fewer side reactions (especially flushing and liver effects). Even more important, it can be safely combined with statin drugs.

It is important to undergo liver function studies and creatine kinase (CK) blood levels for muscular effect when taking a statin and/or niacin. Liver function can be altered and muscular changes can occur but are not very common and are reversible. There are other agents (cholestyramine, colestipol, and colesevelam) that can bind bile acid resin and reduce LDL but are not as effective as the statins and niacin. Gemfibrozil (Lopid) and fenofibrate (Tricor) are fibric acids that can decrease triglycerides and increase HDL. Gemfibrozil may interfere with the catabolism (breakdown) of statins and if combined may predispose to myopathy (muscle changes in the body). Fenofibfrate does not do this and may be safer with a statin drug combination. Another agent called ezetimibe (Zetia) inhibits the intestinal absorption of cholesterol. It is important to realize that correcting the risk factors (abnormal lipids, smoking, exercise, weight reduction, and hypertension) not only prevent coronary heart disease but also may cause regression of plaques in the coronary arteries.

Herbal therapies are escalating in the United States. It is important to be aware of adverse effects, doses, and potential interactions with prescription medications. Nearly one in five taking prescription medications also use herbs. Patients often fail to mention to doctors that they are taking these herbal preparations, which are marketed without proof of efficacy or safety by the Food and Drug Administration (FDA). There are many listed for cardiovascular disease such as danshen, dong quai, garlic, gingko (biloba), ginseng, hawthorn, hellebore; horse chestnut, yohimbe and St. John's wort. The evidence for efficacy of these is very weak. Unfortunately, many of these cause platelet dysfunction and bleeding. If such patients are also taking aspirin, warfarin (Coumadin) Plavix, or vitamin E, they are more prone to hemorrhage. Cases of cerebral hemorrhage have been reported. At present there are ongoing studies with many herbs that may clarify their action and value. Recent studies were inconclusive that the antioxidant vitamins E and C may prevent cardiovascular events. Vitamin D has been shown to play a significant role in the cardiovascular system. Many people are found to have a low level of vitamin D resulting in part from more indoor activities and the avoidance of sunshine. Chronic deficiency is important in the pathophysiology of coronary heart disease, hypertension, heart failure, and other cardiovascular disorders. A blood test can screen for this deficiency.

A friend took vitamins A, B, C, D, E, F, and G, and still looked like H.

Co-enyzme Q10 has been recommended or studied in numerous conditions but remains controversial as a treatment. There is some evidence that statin drugs may reduce Q10 levels and produce muscle weakness. Limited studies have shown that Q10 can decrease muscle pain severity and allow more patients to benefit from statin drugs, especially those who do not have elevated CK.

A faith healer came to town and told the congregation if anyone had a problem to come forward. A lady on crutches, Mrs. Brown, came up and said, "I have arthritis and would like to walk without crutches." He said, "Go behind that curtain and pray, and I will have you walking." Next a Mr. Jones came up and said, "I can't speak clearly." The faith healer said, "Go behind the curtain, and I will have you speaking clearly." He told the congregation to pray for these poor souls and asked Mrs. Brown to throw one of her crutches over the screen. She did and the congregation gave a big sigh. Next he told her to throw the other crutch over, and she did. The congregation was amazed. "Now, Mr. Jones," the faith healer said, "Say something." There was a pause. Then, in a slurring voice Mr. Jones said, "Mrs. Brown just fell on her ass."

After a heart attack patients should be on a prevention program that includes cardiac rehabilitation. All the risk factors should be controlled. Weight and exercise are very important. After discharge, many patients should be on a statin drug, 81-mg coated aspirins, ACE-inhibitors, and beta-blockers. Those who have a drug-eluting (coated) stent should take Plavix at least a year.

There are many other diseases of the heart that involve valves, the pericardium membrane around the heart, and the cardiac muscle. Irregularities of the heart with or without disease are also often referred to as *heart attacks*. However, the words *heart attack* should be used only when a coronary artery suddenly becomes blocked, and the part of the heart muscle that receives blood from that artery dies.

I am thankful that I am in good health and excellent shape.

A doctor told a sixty-year-old man he was in excellent shape for his age. "How old was your father when he died?" he asked. The man said, "Who said my father is dead? He is eighty-five-years-old and works every day." The doctor asked, "How old was your grandfather when he died?" The man said, "Who said he was dead? In fact, he plans to get married in two weeks." The doctor said, "Why does he want to do that at his age?" The man said, "Who says he wants to."

My only illnesses have been hemorrhoids, kidney stones, a reaction to a tick bite, and prostatitis. I planned my hemorrhoidectomy without any of my colleagues being aware of this. My surgeon, a proctologist, was referred to in Charleston as the Rear Admiral. I went to St. Francis Hospital, and if all went well, the following morning I was to go home. The hemorrhoidectomy was uneventful. The next morning I got up to shave. When I stood I had a severe headache and nausea. Immediately on lying down, these symptoms cleared. I again attempted to get up. The symptoms returned, and I realized that I was having a spinal headache. For the next several days, I could not raise my head even fifteen degrees above the pillow before the symptoms returned. It was impossible lying flat and receiving opiate medications to have a bowel movement. As a result, I had to have enemas administered through the very raw and painful area. Since I could not stand, I had to use a bedpan. This made me appreciate my patients even more. Since then, I have never ordered a bedpan.

Two young priests ran out of gasoline on the highway. They went to a service station that gave them a bedpan in which to carry the gasoline. Their bishop drove by with a friend and saw them pouring gas from the bedpan into the gas tank. "Isn't it wonderful," the bishop said, "that our young priests believe in miracles?"

When finally I did have a bowel movement, it was like passing ground glass. I gave out such a yell I probably wakened the whole hospital.

After two weeks, I decided to go home to die. On the way, I again had a very severe headache. My wife wanted to turn back, but I insisted that we go directly home. It took twelve more days for my symptoms to clear. However, I had another problem. Every time I farted there was a whistling sound. I went back to work at the hospital, and while examining patients I sometimes would have this involuntary whistling sound. My patients wondered what was going on. When I went to play golf, every time I leaned over to tee my ball, I whistled. A friend, Dick Schreadly, after he heard my "whistling" on the golf course, nodded and said, "Whistle while you work."

It took me three months to recover from the hemorrhoidectomy. I wrote Blue Cross/Blue Shield that it should not be listed as a minor operation but a major one.

I was playing golf with a urologist friend, and I asked him about a patient in the hospital who had a kidney stone. He said that he was doing well. I said, "Those stones are very painful." He said, "You should know because you had one." I answered that I never had a kidney stone. Well, that night at 10:00 P.M., I had sudden pain in my back that radiated to my bladder. My wife was so anxious that she could not call the urologist, so I had to stagger from bed to make the call. He said, "I was only kidding you this afternoon." "Yes, you were kidding, but I have one now."

I was admitted to the hospital and eventually had to be cystoscoped (direct visualization of the bladder and urinary tract) because the stone was not moving. The cystoscopy room was just off the hallway. The urologist brought out this long instrument, and I asked him what he was going to do with that? He said "I am just going to ease it in your penis to the bladder." He did, and then had a nurse assistant hold it while he went out into the hallway and gossiped. All those walking past could see me.

The stone would not pass and could not be retrieved. After two weeks, I was sent home. A friend said, "Why don't you drink a few bottles of beer?" After drinking two, I passed the stone. I never knew that such a small thing could give so much pain. A pathologist friend examined the stone, and knowing that I was a cardiologist, he called it a "cholesterol" stone. That wasn't the case.

Another time I went with a patient to look at a small island he wanted to sell. After returning to my office, I noticed that there was a little black spot on my penis. I pulled it off, and then it began to bleed. It was a tick. After about an hour my penis became very red and swollen. The urologist gave me some medication, but a small abscess formed. This was drained. Following this, a small cyst developed. This also had to be removed and with the stitching my penis bent, and I could not pee straight. This upset my wife, as I often missed the commode. After several weeks, things straightened out.

My daughter has a country home and on a Fourth of July we visited her. I went into the nearby woods and that night began itching all over. Chiggers, so-called red bugs, were all over me. Someone told me I should use a cigarette lighter to burn them off. I didn't think that was wise. Someone else suggested coating them with clear nail polish. That worked best, but I ended up with many large blisters that had to be incised by a dermatologist.

My final illness was prostatitis (inflammation of the prostate gland), which took several weeks to clear. I was given many antibiotics, some of which caused side reactions. It was difficult working and lecturing under these conditions. I finally recovered, and since then I have been in good health.

An elderly patient was in a doctor's waiting room, and he asked a young man who was also waiting, "Why have you come to see the doctor?" The young man stuttered, "I have a so-so-sore throat. Wh-Why did you come?" The elderly man said, "I have a prostate problem." The young man asked, "Wh-Wh-What is that?" The elderly man said, "This is difficult to explain, but I pee like you talk."

I had four accidents. The first, mentioned earlier, was when I broke my rib. The second was when I was playing golf with a radiologist from Roper Hospital, and he shanked a golf ball that hit my knee. That night I limped while making rounds at St. Francis Hospital. The radiologist there saw me and said

I must have an X-ray. The radiologist who hit me was told this the next day. He called and said, "You didn't even have the courtesy to come to me for an X-ray, since I am the one who hit you?" I answered in jest, "I plan to sue you."

The third accident occurred when I was coming home from a late call, and a car driving very fast hit me on the driver's side as I made a left-hand turn. The driver was speeding on the wrong side of the street; he was heading to the airport and was late. At that time we did not have seat belts, and I found myself out on the sidewalk but thankfully with no injuries. The fourth accident occurred while I was going to a hotel to give a talk. I had seen on television that a small car, the Capri, was built for the sexy European. So I had bought one. A large jeep van ran a stop sign and hit my Capri, spinning me into a telephone pole. Fortunately I was wearing a seat belt and did not sustain any injuries. The car was a total loss, and I never again bought a small car. These were four *through the back door* experiences.

Physicians work long hours and need to take time off to smell the roses. It's important that they have periodic physical examinations and follow what they preach. They should have hobbies and make time for relaxation.

CHAPTER 8
FAMILY AND FRIENDS
This Is What Makes Life

Athena and I have been married for sixty-two years. We have three daughters, eight grandchildren, and nine great grandchildren. We have been blessed to have good health and a wonderful family. Athena has been very active in our medical association and in our church. She is a past president of the Charleston Medical Alliance and also of the State Alliance for doctors' spouses. Twelve years ago, she started the Father Trivelas Library in our Orthodox Christian Church. It now has over 5,000 religious books, all contributed by parishioners. The library is completely computerized and books can be taken out. In addition, there is a bookstore and reference book section. Athena is the director and our daughter Hope the codirector. Athena is past president of the Philoptochos Society, a benevolent society of our church, and she also coordinates a prayer chain. For many years she was director of a Bible study group.

Our family has been active in the Orthodox Christian Church. I was appointed as an archon of the ecumenical patriarchate. This is one of the greatest honors a layperson can receive in our church. I am also a member of the Archbishop Iakovos leadership 100 endowed fund and have served on the Archdiocese Council of the Greek Orthodox Church of North and South America. I am very proud to be an American and also very proud of my Greek heritage. Before the schism in 1054, all Christian churches were one. The Orthodox Christian Church went east and the Catholic Church, west. Our patriarch is head of the Orthodox Church, and the pope the head of the Catholic Church. Our services are very similar. In our Orthodox church we have archbishops, metropolitans, bishops, and priests. Our patriarch is housed in Constantinople, Turkey. Our priests are permitted to marry only before ordination. Father Alexander Karloutsos, protopresbyter of the Ecumenical Patriarchate, is a wonderful person who has dedicated his life to the Orthodox Church. In addition to serving with the patriarch, he also has a parish, Kimisis Tis Theotokou, Greek Orthodox Church of the Hamptons in South Hampton, New York. Athena and I had the privilege of attending one of his services. It was indeed spiritually fulfilling. Father Alex and his wife, Xanthi, are instrumental in making America aware of our wonderful Orthodox Christian Church.

Our priest gave a sermon on forgiveness. At the end of his sermon, he asked the parishioners to stand if they plan to forgive their enemies. I was the only one who did not stand. The priest was surprised and asked, "You do not have any enemies?" I said, "No, I am eighty-eight years-old, and I have outlived all of the SOBs."

Athena is active in caring for our yard. The grass has to be cut, leaves collected, and shrubbery trimmed. Since it was difficult to get help, I decided to purchase a riding mower, and cut the grass and collect the leaves. One day it was very cold, and I dressed with several sweaters and a hat and began to cut the grass. After a while I called Athena to get me goggles to protect my eyes. Next I became concerned that the loud noise would affect my hearing, so I had Athena go and purchase earplugs. My friends would drive by and want to talk, but I could not hear them. One time a chauffeured car stopped with a lady in the backseat. She was impressed with our yard and asked how much I charged. I said, "Nothing." She was surprised. I said, "I have the privilege of sleeping with the lady of the house."

My yard work didn't continue for long because one Saturday my three daughters came, and I sadly said, "Look, all my friends are playing golf, and I have to work in the yard." They began to cry and told their mother that I should be playing golf. This was the last of my yard work. I got out of it *through the back door.*

We always made time for our daughters regardless of how busy we were. Often I would come home for dinner and then go back to the hospital to complete my work. It is very important that families eat and pray together. For several years, I would leave early in the morning while my daughters were asleep with their hair in curlers. I would return at night, and they would again be sleeping with curlers in their hair. When I saw them without curlers, I didn't recognize them.

Each year we took our family on vacation to different resorts. On the way we'd stop at motels that had a swimming pool. Each daughter would ask me to watch her as she dove and swam. We visited such places as Cherokee, North Carolina, and Gatlinburg, Tennessee.

Each of our daughters is unique. Hope was born in Philadelphia. When Athena was in labor, I was on medical duty at the Republican Convention and the Philadelphia Inquirer ran the following article.

PHILADLEPHIA INQUIRER
July 1, 1948

IN OUR TOWN
By Don Fairbairn

Dr. Peter C. Gazes, assistant chief resident at Philadelphia General Hospital, was on medical duty at Convention Hall last week. He got a ticket for his wife, Athena, an ardent Deweyite, in the balcony for Thursday's balloting. In the midst of Ballot No. 2, she heard the beat of stork wings, was rushed to Lying-In Hospital. Dr. Gazes kept calling to ask how she was doing. She kept replying, "How is Dewey doing? I do hope he wins." Baby arrived on Friday afternoon. If a boy, they planned to name him Dewey. It was a 7-pound girl. They named her Hope.

This interview was somewhat different than he reported. Athena was at the hospital in labor, and I was nervous for fear I would not get there in time for the delivery. Also, we did not plan that if we had a boy to name him Dewey.

Agnes Scott is an all girls' school in Atlanta, Georgia. Hope received her college degree from there. I always sent her a prescription blank with this on it: "Remember that in thirty minutes before the altar you can determine your lifestyle." I would add a five-dollar bill with this note. On Father's Day at Agnes Scott, I was allowed to visit the dormitory. Many girl students in unison repeated the writing on my notes. Apparently, Hope let them read my letters. During her stay there she met Michael Grayson, a Georgia Tech student whom she later married.

Hope became known as our actress. She participated in many elementary, high school, and college plays and now performs in local theaters. She recently completed "Master Class," the story of the opera singer Maria Callas after she could no longer sing and taught singing. This was a two-hour monologue, and Hope did extremely well. It was received with acclaim. She did at least twelve performances at a local theater and another twelve with the Piccolo Festival, a part of the Spoleto Festival. The Spoleto Festival is a nationally known arts festival held in Charleston for the last thirty-three years. People come from all over to see plays, musicals, operas, dancing, and many other performing arts. The founder of the festival was opera composer Gian Carlo Menotti. He organized the festival first in Spoleto, Italy, then came to America and chose Charleston as the site for a second festival. The two were marketed Festival of the Two Worlds. We had the opportunity about fifteen years ago to visit the little town of Spoleto, which is about seventy miles from Rome. This was a wonderful small arts town with many playhouses. In fact, one of the hotels was named the Charleston.

Hope has been very active in our Orthodox Christian Church. She was the first female president of the Church Council. As I mentioned, she also volunteers with her mother in operating the Father Trivelas Library. Both Hope and her mother have been president of the Charleston Medical Alliance and also the State Alliance for doctors' spouses. Hope served eight years on the National Alliance Medical Council. Her husband, Michael, is a cardiologist, and they have two boys and a girl. One of their sons, Peter, is a fellow in rheumatology at Boston University. His brother Clay is a tax attorney practicing in downtown Charleston. Peter went to medical school at the Medical University of South Carolina and Clay received his law degree from the University of South Carolina in Columbia. Clay spent one year in New York studying tax law. Hope's daughter, Athena, named after her grandmother, graduated from Florida State and is now married. She is the assistant manager of a downtown Charleston ladies clothing store.

My middle daughter, Cathy, is an extremely active person. When she was one-year old, I slipped down twenty stairs holding her in my arms. Since then I never go downstairs in stocking feet. Fortunately, neither one of us was hurt. When she was three, I took her to the zoo and she screamed, "Daddy, look at that large puppy!" I turned and saw it was a buffalo. At four, we went to a department store to buy her mother a present. She began squirming and wanted to go to the ladies room. I had never been in the ladies room, but the sales lady, who knew me, said "I will be glad to take her there." When she returned I asked Cathy, "Did you thank Mrs. Jones?" She said, "Why should I? She had to go too."

Before one of my talks, a lady asked me if I ever get nervous. I said, "Absolutely not." Then she said, "Well then, why are you in the ladies room?"

Once I had to go to a medical meeting in Philadelphia. Since Athena's parents were still living there, I took Cathy. This was an overnight train ride. All night long, at every station, she pulled down the curtain to see if we had arrived in Philadelphia. Everyone on the platform could see us. In the morning, we had breakfast, and the conductor was very helpful. He showed her how to use a napkin. He tied a knot and placed the knot under her chin and just under her blouse. She was thrilled with this. On arriving in Philadelphia, we went to my in-laws' home. One night it was snowing heavily, and I borrowed my father-in-law's hat to wear to a medical meeting. It was a very small hat, too small in fact, and everyone thought I was some sort of country hick.

During this visit, Cathy received many gifts for herself and her sisters. She had a large bag filled with them. At the Philadelphia Thirtieth Street train station on our way home, she fell just before getting on the train. The gifts were scattered all over the platform. My mother-in-law and I had to scramble to pick them up; otherwise Cathy would not leave.

There came a time when Cathy had to have her baby teeth pulled. This was done in the operating room, and I went in with the oral surgeon. She looked up at me and said, "Daddy, what are you doing in this operating room pretending you are a doctor?"

A lady went to the dentist for a tooth extraction. She said, "I hate this painful procedure. I would rather have a pregnancy with labor pains." The dentist said, "Lady, make up your mind, so I will know how to tilt the table."

All off my daughters took piano lessons. Cathy, however, had a problem with rehearsals. She would begin playing by memory, but then would forget and keep repeating. Finally, she'd grab the sheet music and play from it. She also performed in many plays. During one Shakespearean play, she tripped over a sword backstage before going on and had a cut on her leg that required stitches.

Her first husband was a dentist. They had two boys, John and Arthur. John is in Chicago in graphic design and does TV commercials for Budweiser beer. He recently married one of his associates.

Arthur is a doctor at the University of North Carolina at Chapel Hill and is specializing in maternal and fetal medicine. He married one of his attending physicians who is also an ob-gyn. It's interesting how they met. She was his attending staff doctor and helped him deliver a baby. At the same time, she showed him how to do a circumcision. During the operation, he looked up at her and asked for a date. They now have two daughters. Cathy taught school for about twenty years. She lost her husband at a very young age and remained single during her teaching career. She dated occasionally but did not find anyone she especially liked.

One day I was playing golf with Ty Cline, a close friend. Ty had graduated from Clemson University and became a professional baseball player in the big leagues. He played for such teams as Atlanta, Montreal, San Francisco, and Cincinnati. He played in the World Series with Pete Rose and Johnny Bench. Ty's wife had died after a long illness. During one golf game, Ty asked me, "Do you know a nice girl I could go out with? I find it lonely going back to my home."

I told him I had just the right girl in mind—my daughter Cathy. He was surprised. I gave him her telephone number. This was on a Tuesday, and he did not call her until Sunday. He waited because he has three daughters and wanted to tell them of his desire to date. When he called Cathy, they spoke for forty-five minutes. They had never met. The next day they met over a cup of coffee. A year later, they married.

This couple was celebrating their thirtieth anniversary at a party with their friends. As usual, the men gathered in one room and the ladies in another. The wife went over and slapped her husband, "That's for being a poor lover for thirty years," she said. After awhile, he went over and slapped her. "Why did you do that?" she asked. Her husband said, "That's for knowing the difference."

A son asked his mother, "How old are you? How much do you weigh? How tall are you? Why did Daddy divorce you?" She said, "None of your business." The son found her driver's license and said, "I know everything about you. You are fifty-two-years-old, weigh 120 pounds, are five-foot-two-inches tall, and Daddy divorced you because you made an F in sex."

Joanne is my youngest daughter. Every time Athena and I went on a trip, we'd get a call from her pediatrician that Joanne had fallen off a swing, broken her collarbone, or had some other accident. She went one year to Salem College and transferred to the College of Charleston. I insisted that she graduate before getting married. Her husband (Blount) is a cardiologist and practices with my other son-in-law. In fact, they are my competitors since I practiced cardiology at the Medical University of South Carolina.

Blount was the only student I ever taught who fell asleep in my class. He is a member of the St. Andrews Episcopal Church. Athena and I insisted that their family go to one church, so Joanne joined the Episcopal Church. At present Joanne is conducting a very large Bible study that includes some

250 people. The study is titled Drawing Near to God. She's given speeches in many states and has published a 365-day devotional book, also titled *Drawing Near to God*. They have two daughters and one son. One daughter, Catherine, is married to an arborist (Gregg) and the other, Hope, is married to an orthopedist (Chris). Many in our family are named Hope after my mother. Their son Billy is an arborist and works with Greg. He recently had a destination wedding (away from the bride's hometown) to a lovely girl, Emily, in, Waynesville, North Carolina. Now that we have cardiologists, rheumatologist, obstetricians, orthopedist, lawyers, a professional ball player, and arborists (tree surgeons), I want to open a common office with all of them with a sign "We treat you from the womb to the tomb." Perhaps I can convince the ball player to become a mortician.

My daughter Joanne wanted a poodle. She'd call me at the office several times per day a ask, "Daddy, are you thinking about the poodle?" Finally, I told her mother to go ahead and buy a poodle, which my daughter named Taffy.

This man told another, "I hear your wife is running around with your best friend." He went home and shot his dog.

A salesman approached a house. He saw a dog. He asked a man working in the yard, "Does your dog bite?" The man said, "No." The salesman went on, and the dog nearly tore him apart. The salesman turned, "I thought your dog didn't bite." "Yes," the man said. "But that's not my dog."

Later Joanne wanted a horse, and she did the same thing, calling me at the office. We finally bought her a Palomino. The horse appeared to have a large abdomen and spindly legs, but we were not aware of anything wrong. One morning at breakfast, I had a call from the stable that I was the proud father of a baby colt. We didn't know the mare was pregnant.

Joanne wanted to show all the neighborhood children the colt, so that night I gathered all the children in my station wagon and headed to the stable. I opened the gate and pointed the car lights on the very cute colt. We forgot to close the gate. Expensive horses were leaving the stable. I had to run with all the kids to corral them before they reached the highway. One man with a rifle came out and called me a horse thief. Fortunately, the children and I managed to corral all the horses. The children's families were concerned because we did not get them home until midnight.

Joanne's daughter Catherine wanted a horse and asked me to persuade her mother. I told her to use her mother's tactic for getting her horse—just call her mother several times every day, and ask if she was thinking about a horse. It worked, and her parents eventually bought one.

I was a member of the Lions Club, and one year I was given ten raffle tickets to sell. Rather than doing this, I bought them myself. The tickets were for a rodeo on Sunday afternoon. I took the entire family and at the end of the rodeo, a prize was drawn for a Shetland pony and saddle. What a surprise, I won it! There we were on a Sunday afternoon walking a pony down the street and not knowing what we were going to do with it. A state senator friend saw me and said he would take the pony to his farm and that I could bring my daughters there at any time to ride. This was another *through the back door.*

A man had two sons, one a pessimist and the other an optimist. On Christmas Day the pessimist came downstairs, and his father said, "Son, I have a bicycle for you." The son said, "Daddy, that bicycle will not last long." He mentioned several faults. Next, his optimistic son came down, and he was led to a room full of horse manure. "Son, this is your Christmas present, and the son said, "Thank you, Daddy. This is the greatest present I ever received." He began digging in the horse manure, and said, "I know that there must be a pony here somewhere."

I was on a winning streak. After the pony, I won a Hi-Fi stereo set at the annual South Carolina Medical Association meeting. Next I won a color TV. My secretary's husband came in the office one day to sell a $25 raffle ticket for a Cadillac sponsored by the Elks Club. I held the ticket for a few moments but decided not to buy it. He said since I had touched the ticket he would buy it, and he won the Cadillac. There went my luck.

My family and I often went together to different activities, including weddings. One time I was in a tuxedo, and Athena and the girls were in long dresses. After a beautiful church wedding, as we began to leave the church, a heavy rain developed. I took each of my family with an umbrella to the car. When I finally got all of them in the car, I had trouble closing the umbrella. When I thought it was closed, I got into the car. Suddenly the umbrella snapped open, and we all got wet. I tried again to close the umbrella. I couldn't do it. Usually I am very calm, but this time I folded the umbrella, opened the car trunk and angrily threw it in. I could hear it pop open as soon as I closed the trunk. By this time I was drenched and very unhappy.

Athena often went with me on medical trips. A private jet took us to Spartanburg, South Carolina, for a consult with an executive's wife. He was the CEO of a dress company. At the airport we were met with two limousines. One took Athena to the dress factory, and the other took me to the hospital. After my consult, I met Athena back at the plane. The plane was stacked with boxes. They had told her to pick out dresses for herself and our three daughters. With all of these gifts, how could I now charge for my consult? We returned to Charleston and in the confusion of getting all the boxes of dresses out of the plane my wife left our car keys. The jet had taken off, and the private airport manager called for its return.

An ideal husband is one who can make love all night long, and in the morning, turn into a credit card.

I had time to consult at Spartanburg because there then was a strike by workers at the Medical University Hospital. An attempt was being made to unionize them. They picketed the hospital and tried to keep us out. I had to admit the chairman of county council to the hospital with a heart attack. He showed me a list of the workers' demands. The strike finally was settled with few demands being met. Because of the strike the City of Charleston imposed a curfew and my daughter Hope had to have an early wedding instead of the one planned for 8:00 P.M.

A Greek ship came to Charleston, and I was asked to see the captain's wife, who had a cardiac problem. Afterward he invited Athena and me for dinner on the ship. The food was excellent, especially the codfish. In Greek the word for codfish (*bakaliaros*) and the sweet baklava dessert sound very much alike. By mistake I told him that my favorite food was baklava when I intended to say codfish. All night they kept bringing me baklava. As we were leaving, the captain gave us a large box full of it. He also gave us a big bottle of sweet Greek wine. At home Athena poured the wine into empty grape juice bottles. We later took a trip, leaving Athena's mother to take care of the children. When we came back, they all met us at the door and told us what their *Yia Yia* (grandmother in Greek) had done. One morning they got up late and did not have time to eat breakfast. Yia Yia insisted that they at least have some juice and gave them what she thought was grape juice. At school they got dizzy and had to be sent home.

Two Jewish men were in a Greek restaurant and one said, "I wonder if there are any Greek Jews?" They asked the waiter and he said, "I will ask the chef." He returned and said, "The chef says no Greek Jews." They next asked the owner. He said, "We have no Greek Jews, but we do have orange juice, tomato juice, and other kinds."

Another time, I tried to make the dessert cherries jubilee. I poured brandy over the cherries and tried to light it. It didn't catch, and I kept pouring on more brandy. It turned out that the brandy had to be heated before lighting. We ate the dessert anyway, with ice cream. We were all woozy.

We always celebrated Christmas at home. One year, though, we decided to take the girls and our gifts to my in-laws in Philadelphia. When we arrived, it was snowing heavily. I went outside with my brother-in-law (Peter) and began throwing snowballs. I packed one very tight and threw it. He ducked, and it went through a neighbor's window. I was very embarrassed to tell the lady that I had done this.

When the girls were asleep, my brother-in-law and I decided to erect a playhouse that was one of their presents. The directions were very confusing, as they usually are. After drinking about a pint of scotch we completed the job by 5:00 A.M. in the morning. I told my wife from now on any toys she bought had to be assembled beforehand.

Speaking of Christmas – Three men were killed in an automobile accident, and St. Peter said, "You can come in only if you have something related to Christmas." The first one pulled out a cigarette lighter and lit it. That resembled candles so he went in. The second pulled out keys from his pocket and rattled them like Christmas bells so he was allowed in. The third pulled out a pair of girl's panties. St. Peter said, "What is that?" He said, "It's Carol's." So he went on in.

A few days before Christmas, a friend who operates the famous Robert's restaurant in Charleston, which has excellent food and where Robert himself sings (he has a wonderful voice), came to the back door of my home to bring me a gift. It was a very cold night. I was shaving and went to the door in a flimsy short robe. My father-in-law was in the kitchen and not realizing that I was outside closed the back door. I still had the shaving lather on my face. As I turned around I noticed the door was closed. I rang the doorbell but my father-in-law who can't hear well did not answer it. Robert had to leave for his restaurant, and I was embarrassed to go to my neighbors with half of my body exposed and lather on my face, which had formed a cake of ice. About twenty minutes later my wife came from the back bedroom and heard the doorbell. When I came in I looked like a frozen popsicle.

Before another Christmas, Athena and I were in New York in Saks Fifth Avenue. She saw silk ties on sale for $25 and insisted that I buy at least three. A few days before Christmas, Athena and I were going to a party, and I decided to wear one of my new ties. After tying a Windsor knot, I began to laugh. Athena looked and saw that the tie came down just about six inches. We had bought the ties in the boy's department. I had to buy vests to cover the short ties.

Besides Christmas, my family enjoys New Years and Easter. Athena and I rise early on New Year's Day to prepare *Loukoumades*, a tradition handed down by our parents. Batter is mixed with yeast and allowed to rise for about an hour. Canola oil is heated in a pot. I squeeze the batter in my left hand, scoop a spoonful with my right, and put it in the oil. It pops up to the surface and then browns. It is important to get the consistency just right. This can only be achieved by feel and frequent practice. If the batter is too loose the Loukoumades will not be round and will have many extensions. If the batter is too tight the inside will not cook. The amount of liquid and flour according to feel is most important to get the proper consistency. I am trying to get my daughters to get the feeling for in the future it will be their duty to carry on the tradition. After the Loukoumades are cooked, they look like the hole of a doughnut. Everyone starts with about ten on a plate covered with honey, powdered white sugar, sesame seeds, and ground pecans. Often we have them with feta cheese. I started using only one recipe that makes about four dozen. Now with all our grandchildren and great grandchildren, I have to make six times as much. I often call them "honey puffs or Greek doughnuts." Occasionally I use whole-wheat flour. These are tougher but better for your heart.

Many Greeks have recipes but they do not know the exact amount of ingredients. My friend Tone's mother-in-law makes terrific pitas. One day my father-in-law and I decided to make an apple pita. Once in the oven, we noticed that the pita rose 2 to 3 inches. Pitas are usually flat. She did not tell us to use plain flour, and we used self-rising instead. We ended up with an apple cake. I recommend *Popular Greek Recipes* compiled by the Greek ladies of the Philoptochos Society of Charleston, South Carolina.

Easter is a very special time for our family. The time of occurrence is based on the Julian calendar, not the Western Gregorian. It must be after the Jewish holiday of the Passover, and it must be on the first Sunday after the first full moon after the spring equinox. About every four years it coincides with American Western Easter. Because of the differences in time of occurrence many do not consider Greeks as Christians. Of all the Christian feast days, Easter is the greatest time for food, feasting, and celebration in the Greek Orthodox Christian faith. Red-dyed hard-boiled eggs are symbolic of Greek Easter. Tradition says the Virgin Mother Mary dyed eggs this color to celebrate the Resurrection of Christ and the celebration of life. On the Easter Sunday meal each member of our family receives a red-dyed hard-boiled egg and attempts to crack each other's egg. This is to symbolize Christ's breaking from the tomb. The person whose egg remains unbroken is assured good luck for the rest of the year. The main dish is lamb served in honor of the Lamb of

God who was sacrificed and rose again on Easter. I roast the spiced lamb over charcoal on the outside rotisserie. We like it well done so it takes several hours. I constantly baste it with herbs, lemon juice, and olive oil while I am sipping wine and eating Greek Easter cookies (*koulourakia*). Octopus, calamari, rice pilaf, fish roe dip (*taramosalata*), and rice stuffed grape leaves (*dolmades*) are favorites. *Tsoureki* is the traditional sweet bread of Easter. *Mageritsa* is the traditional food on the Resurrection table. It is a creamy, lemony, soup made from the lamb's sweetmeats. *Kokoretsi* consists of lamb and all of the insides, chopped intestines, sweetbreads, hearts, lung, and/or kidney. It is marinated in lemon, olive oil, oregano, and seasoned with salt and paper. It reminds me of haggis in Scotland.

We had two major robberies at our home. The first occurred when our family went on vacation. On returning at night, we saw that all the front curtains were missing. At first we thought that Athena's mother took them down for cleaning. Entering the front room, we saw that all the furniture was gone. Athena's jewelry and our silver were gone. In one of the bedrooms, there was a broken window and blood on the bed. The robber must have been small to get through the broken panes. I decided I would be a detective, and I checked the emergency rooms of hospitals to see if someone came in with abdominal skin cuts. We did not find any clues. Athena thought that a woman was involved, for they took a mop and an old dishtowel. Six months later, I was at the hospital with my dying mother, when I was notified that they had caught the burglars. We had to identify our belongings. Our stereo set had been painted green. I recognized it because one of the cabinets had Greek records. The jewelry and my twelve bottles of Chivas Regal scotch were not recovered. The burglars were a middle-aged lady and two high school students. Their home was furnished with stolen items. There were television sets, toasters, chairs, and other kinds of furniture. It is interesting how they were caught. At the Isle of Palms (a barrier island) a car with a lady and two boys drove into a service station with a trailer full of furniture at 2:00 A.M. in the morning. The sheriff happened to be there and asked them what they were doing. The lady said they had just moved to Charleston and were looking for a place to rent. He took their license plate number. The next day a local citizen called that his house at the Isle of Palms had been burglarized.

Our next robbery happened a few days after hurricane Hugo hit Charleston. That night we went to an annual family party. Our alarm was not activated because it was not working properly. On returning home, we came into the kitchen through the garage. I stopped momentarily to look at a football game on the kitchen TV but then decided to go to the bedroom. Athena stayed in the kitchen. I had to pass through a sitting room to a hallway, and I saw someone running in the hallway. He had a box in one hand and a mink coat draped over his shoulder. As he turned to go out the front door, the coat fell off. I could see that he was a man with brown hair, but I could not see what he had in his other hand. Athena called 911 and told the dispatcher to block the Country Club entrance. They told her not to be frantic for they knew what to do. I ran after him around the back of the house, but he escaped across the golf course. It is amazing that he could cross the golf course so rapidly because the course was being rebuilt and there were gaping holes everywhere. The patrol came but they did not block the golf course entrance. Most of my wife's important jewelry and silver were stolen. Even though I described as much of him as possible, they never caught him. In a way this was a *through the back door* experience. I foolishly ran after him not knowing what he had in his hand. It could have been a gun.

With four friends, I invested in Folly Beach. We bought all the commercial property on the front beach. There were many buildings, a small hotel, and a very large pier with a dance hall. Net income easily covered our mortgage. Instead, we decided to tear down all the buildings except the pier and replace them with prestressed concrete structures. We added a concrete wall and wide walkway the length of the project. To do this we had to borrow more money from the bank. We and our wives signed the note. That first summer the highway to Folly Beach was being widened to four lanes. This limited the number of people going to the beach. Our employees found ways to steal money. The bank had to foreclose. It came to me for the interest and the money it lost by foreclosure. The bank advised me to collect from the others, since I had signed the note individually. The others refused to help, and it took me ten years to pay this debt. This was definitely a *through the back door*, but it taught me a good lesson. Unless you can participate in a project, you should not invest in it, and certainly do not sign the note I did. It is wrong also to gamble and mortgage your home to get investment money. My friends now refer to the Folly Beach as *Pete's Folly*.

These two couples were playing bridge. The husband of one of the couples was bidding strangely, and his wife was becoming mad. After awhile he got up to go to the bathroom, and his wife said, "This is the first time tonight I know what he is holding in his hand."

I had two brothers, Jimmy and Pat, and two sisters, Margaret and Nicky. Pat was very quiet and obeyed my father, but Jimmy was just the opposite.

Our father did not allow us to go swimming under the Ashley Bridge. Jimmy decided to go swimming in the nude with his friends. My father became aware of this and headed to the bridge with a whip. He could not drive across because of stock car races that were held at Folly Beach on Sunday, and traffic was bumper to bumper. Once he arrived on the west side, Jimmy's friends called out that his father was coming. Jimmy came out of the water and found that they had tied up all of his clothing in knots. He ran across the bridge nude with my father in hot pursuit. All the cars began honking their horns. Once Jimmy reached the other side, he ran into a friend's house. This was only one of many times that Jimmy angered our father.

During the summer we went several times to Folly Beach. There was a tollgate and once, to avoid paying ten cents, my brother Jimmy and his friend put me in the trunk. At times they purposely left me, and I had to scream for them to return. This caused many to wonder what was happening.

All of the big bands played for dances on Saturday night at the pavilion on the pier. Sunday afternoon there were concerts. One Sunday on the way home from the pier, Jimmy and his friend took me to a drugstore. They bought me some pills that were supposed to be vitamins. That night my urine turned red. I was quite alarmed, for I knew that my Daddy would be angry. The pills were harmless, and the red color soon cleared. Jimmy always did such things, but I know I was his favorite.

Pat was married to Betty and had two sons,Dennis andJerry.Dennis became a dentist and Jerry a banker.Betty ,a wonderful and caring mother, died a few years ago from cancer.It was amazing that she never complained. Jimmy met Ruth at Newberry College.They had one daughter and two sons. Hope became a pharmacist ,Chris a very successful business man and Peter, a musician.Jimmy recently died from cancer at age ninety-one.Being a comedian, at his death bed he said to me "Pete I don't understand the good lord.Why does he want to take me a way during my prime?" Ruth,a kind, sympathetic, person now lives with Hope.

My sisters,Margaret and Nicky,were my greatest supporters. Margaret was a schoolteacher and had two children—Hope, a college teacher, and George, an attorney. Her husband John Morris was an attorney. John was a very affable, kind person who loved to party. I was in Memphis, Tennessee, at a convention and drove with him to Charleston before his marriage to my sister. On the way we stopped in Atlanta to visit with his brother-in-law. At 11:00 A.M. we were Greek dancing and drinking ouzo.

Before moving to Charleston, John was a successful attorney with one of the major firms in Memphis. At that time, he helped one of the restaurant owners with their accounting books. Eventually he bought the restaurant and remodeled it with the name Old Master. A large bust of himself was placed on the top of the restaurant building. He coined a statement the Old Master Says. This was displayed on many billboards and taxicabs. Many went to his restaurant curious to know what the Old Master Says.

Athena and I visited Margaret and John for a weekend. One night they took us to a famous restaurant on the top floor of the Peabody Hotel. There we danced, had cocktails, and enjoyed a wonderful dinner. As was the custom, a cigarette girl came to our table to sell cigarettes. John in his generosity purchased all her wares and told her to go and rest!

Eventually John and his family moved to Charleston. Our daughters referred to him as Uncle Big John. He often took them to the various beaches for outings. Unfortunately, he died at fifty-two. His son, George, has a law office in Charleston and interestingly he opened a restaurant with his daughter, and so followed in his father's footsteps.

Nicky was a secretary at the College of Charleston for many years. She never had any children but did enjoy her nieces and nephews. She also took care of our parents during their last years. Her husband, John Pappas, was a retired attorney from Greece. My siblings lived to age ninety.

My in-laws were great people and very proud of America. They came from Megara, a small town in Greece, about seventy miles from Athens. Their son, Peter, is a retired college professor, My father-in-law had restaurants in Philadelphia and retired in Charleston after my mother-in-law had a heart attack.

At their home they had a small vegetable garden. They were very proud of a small watermelon that they often showed me. A patient gave me two very large watermelons. On the way home, I decided to take one to my in-laws. Just before reaching their home, I had a great idea. I parked short of their home and took one of the large watermelons into their garden. I replaced their small one with this one and spread leaves around it. I then went to the front door and entered to have coffee. After awhile I asked about their small watermelon. My mother-in-law said it was growing every day and that we should see it. When she saw the large watermelon, she began screaming for my father-in-law to come see what happened. My father-in-law saw that I had made a switch. He lived with us after he lost his wife. He died at ninety-seven and never had any illnesses until the heart attack that took his life. Over a twenty-year period, we never had an argument.

Since our home was on the golf course, each morning before the players began, my father-in-law walked the entire course. He knew very little about golf, so I explained that if he saw any golf balls that were not excessively bruised or cut, he should bring them home. One day he waited at the back door until I came from the hospital. He jumped up and said, "I found a bonanza!" In a very large bag, he had many golf balls. Unfortunately, they all had red circles. He had gathered all the balls from the driving range. When I took them back to our pro, we had a great laugh.

The Greek language has words with several different meanings. My Greek is not fluent. Once, when I wanted to compliment my father-in-law, I said to him, "You are *anestitos*." After I left he told Athena that I had called him an insulting word. She began to laugh because she realized that I thought I was saying something good. I thought the word meant calmness and was derived from the word *anesthesia*. It was just the opposite. It meant that he had no feelings. That night when I came home he was waiting outside and he hugged me.

Athena and I include as family many of our friends whom we have met through association with our church, medical profession, and as patients. Several years ago, I gave a lecture at the International Cardiology Congress in Buenos Aires. On my arrival at the speakers lounge, I was told that I could not use my slides because I did not register them the day before. There was no way I could have done that because I had arrived late that night and was not aware of their rules. Fortunately, just ten minutes before my talk, the chairman of the meeting came in and solved my problem by allowing me to use my slides since I arrived late at night. Again this was *through the back door*.

From Argentina we took a side trip to Brazil and visited Rio de Janeiro. In this beautiful city they have many landmarks. One of these is Sugar Loaf Mountain and Corcovado Peak on which stands a huge statue of Christ. Since this is some 3,000 feet up, there were two lifts that went up the mountain. Midway you had to change to go farther up. Suddenly this huge statue of Christ appeared between the clouds. It was amazing.

During our decent, we met a couple, Tone and Pepi Harovas from New York. We became close friends and now, over thirty years later, we still continue to travel together. I became a member of the Hellenic Medical Society of New York and have been on many of their programs in New York and Greece. We have three daughters, and the Harovas have three daughters.

Dr. Harovas has attended my Update Cardiology Program in Charleston for thirty-three years. Through Tone and Pepi, we met Jimmy and Zoe Moshovitas from Washington, DC. Jimmy is a successfu businessman and has ventures worldwide.

We often travel with these two couples and have added a third couple, Mike and Libby Angelides. Mike is a well-known contractor in New York. Several years ago they all came to visit Charleston for three days. On one occasion, we went to see the world famous Angel Oak. This is an unbelievable tree with large branches that are bent and rooted into the ground. The night before our visit, it had rained heavily, and the road had many puddles of water. I was driving the first car with Zoe, Jimmy, and the others were in another car with Athena. I drove through several puddles with no problem but suddenly in one of them my right wheel began to sink and the car could not move. Water began coming in so we all had to scramble to reach high ground. Athena in the other car went to a nearby fire station to get help. A patrol car, a fire truck, towing company, and a medical emergency vehicle all came at one time. The car was pulled out and the motor started, but the car's lights would not go off. In all of the confusion, Jimmy had to go to the bathroom, and we took a picture of him as his pants went down. This was an adventure with friends we will never forget.

I have many golfing buddies. At first I played in a foursome with three other physicians. Invariably one would be late or a beeper would go off on a backswing. I stopped playing for two years, and one day, while walking the golf course, I saw a group of men who were choosing players to play in a team blitz. They argued about which players they wanted, and I told them they sounded like the Little Rascals on TV. The next day, a reporter in the sports section of the newspaper mentioned "the little rascals." He wrote this under his weekly heading called Norineves (*Seven iron* spelled backwards). The name little rascals has stuck to the group to this day.

The beauty of a blitz is that you play with different people each time. Our scores are kept, so they can make up nearly equal teams. The players put a small amount of money in the pot, and the teams play against each other. Through this association I have met a diverse group including architects, lawyers, ministers, service men, and a few doctors. These are the rewards of golf. Some of my golf buddies include: Timothy "Tim" Street was involved in a shipping agency; Richard "Dick" Schreadley is a former *Charleston Evening Post* editor, and when the *News and Courier* and *Evening Post* merged, he was the executive editor for both. Tyrone "Ty" Cline is a former big league ball player, Dominicus

"Dom" Valiunas is a stockbroker, Robert "Bob" Daniel is a former president of the Charleston Coca-Cola bottling Company, Herman Daniell holds a PhD in pharmacology, William "Bill" Zobel is a retired navy admiral, Ernest "Ernie" Chandler is a contractor, Calvin "Cal" East, and Louie Koester III are bankers, Walter "Walt" Bailey is an engineer, Dr. Charles "Charlie" King is a dentist, Stuart Christie is a retired pharmaceutical executive, Dr. Paul Sanders III is a urologist, Claudius "Bud" Watts III is a retired general, John Allison is a surgeon, and Thomas "Tommy" Thorne president of the Woodstock Company and my neighbor for many years.

Besides meeting interesting people, one of the great pleasures of golf is playing different courses. For the past thirty years, I have been going with seven others to the Biltmore Country Club in North Carolina. This is a very beautiful, mountainous course that differs from the Low Country courses in Charleston. We stay in the Biltmore bachelor quarters and have our meals at the club. A story frequently told is that one of the Vanderbilt ladies was a member of the Ashville Country Club but was not allowed to smoke there. She had the Biltmore Forest Country Club built as a place she could smoke and also entertain many of her friends.

A retired doctor lived across the street from me. We played golf together, and he rode a cart with his poodle. I had a caddy. Every hole or two the older doctor would drive near a wooded area and leave the cart. The dog followed him. The old man had a big prostate, and he frequently had to pee. Halfway through the round, he asked my caddy, "How do I stand with Dr. Gazes?" The caddy said, "I don't know. But you're two up on the dog."

A patient who had a tomato farm was a very good golfer. However, as he got older, he could not score in the 70s, so he quit. After five years, I convinced him to play with me. He made par on the first five holes. On the sixth hole he hit the ball in the water. He became so mad he threw his golf bag and clubs in the lake. Then he took off his shoes and socks, and waded into the lake. I thought he had a change of heart, but that was not the case. He found his bag, and from a side pocket he retrieved his car keys. He then threw the bag back into the lake. Golf can be a very frustrating game.

A man was playing golf with his wife and sliced the ball behind a barn. He told his wife he would take a stroke. She said "Honey, don't do that. Open the barn doors on both sides, and you can look through and see the green." He thought that was a great idea. He opened the doors and struck the ball. It went into the barn, hit a rafter, came back, and hit his wife on the head, killing her. Several weeks later he was playing with a friend and again he sliced the ball behind the barn. He told his friend that he would take a stroke. His friend said, "No, don't do that. Open the barn doors on each side, and you can see the green." He said, "Oh, no. The last time I did that I took a double bogey."

I have many friends in Greenville, South Carolina. I first met Alex Kiriakides, president of Atlas Vending Company when he came for a second opinion about forty years ago. He was told he had a damaged heart, but I did not find this to be the case. When I told him my results, he kissed me on my cheeks. All the nurses looked surprised.

Alex was short, overweight with a dark complexion and a gruff voice. Yet, he was kind, gentle, compassionate, and generous. Often he was an anonymous benefactor. One of his favorite projects was an open chapel at Camp Greenville called Pretty Place. As you approach this chapel, you get a feeling of serenity and peace. Through the entrance of the chapel an enormous wooden cross can be seen in the altar. This cross is silhouetted against the background of a light blue sky. On the top of the cross there is a copper cap that glows in the sunlight. At the end of the altar there is a deep valley from which rises a magnificent mountain range. The chapel is open, and its roof is supported by stone columns on which there are plaques with Bible passages. You get a sense of the presence of God in this sacred space.

Over the years Athena and I frequently have seen Alex and his wife Catherine. One New Year's, a group of us were dancing the twist at his home. Outside it was snowing. There we met Nick and Emily Theodore. Nick subsequently became lieutenant governor of South Carolina and served for eight years. The governor was a Republican but Nick was a Democrat.

A banquet was given in my honor before the dedication of the Cardiac Research Building that bears my name. Nick made a few comments, and I got up and said when we met we made history. This was the first time two Greeks met and didn't open a restaurant. Another time we were in New York to celebrate the candidates that received awards from the New York Hellenic Medical Society. Each year a physician and lay award are given. Yanni the musician and composer received the lay award. At that time the actress Linda Evans was his companion. She was very delightful and unassuming. Nick was in New York at the time for political business. He met with us, and he was enthralled with Linda Evans. At his home he has a large portrait of him with his arm around Linda. In 1982, I received the physician award, which was a crystal Steuben apple from the Hellenic Medical Society.

Medical societies often have symbols. I am sometimes asked about the significance of the caduceus and the rod of Asclepius. The caduceus (the wand of Hermes or Mercury, the messenger of gods) is used as an emblem of the U.S. Army Medical Corps. The staff is entwined by two snakes and sometimes surrounded by wings. The official symbol of the medical profession is the staff of Asclepius, which combines a single serpent with the staff as a symbol befitting the god of medicine. Snakes periodically shed their skin, which is a symbol of rebirth and fertility. Another explanation I've heard is that in ancient time mentally ill were shocked by pretending to throw them in a snake pit. The shedding of the snake's skin also may indicate healing.

This snake went into a doctor's office and asked to be fitted with glasses. The doctor said, "I never have done this but let's try." One month later the snake came back and told the doctor, "I now can see everything, and my sex life has improved tremendously." The doctor asked, "How did it affect your sex life?" The snake answered, "All these years, and I never realized I was shacked up with a garden hose."

I became the personal doctor of many of my physician friends. The dean at one time came to see me for an irregular heartbeat. He was very heavy, and I did a stress electrocardiography test. He was on the treadmill, and in the middle of the exam he asked, "What would you do if I died suddenly?" I answered, "I would give you an enema and bury you in a matchbox." I also saw a pathologist who had shortness of breath. He was very obese, too. After I examined him he asked, "What did you find? I said, "You are very fat." He said, "I would like a second opinion." I gave him one. "You are ugly, too," I said.

I have been on the medical staff during every president's term. Dr. McCord was the head of the biochemistry department . One day in his class in biochemistry, he asked a student, "What is the scourge of the South." The student answered, "Jock itch." The correct answer was pellagra. Dr. McCord ran down the hall and got his entire faculty to come back and ask the student this question. When he became president, the Medical School became a Medical University. It now has several schools including dental, allied health sciences, and nursing. Dr. McCord served as president of the Medical University of South Carolina from 1963 to 1975.

I had befriended one of the elevator operators as he always gave me good service. One day President McCord and I got on the elevator. He was to get off on the third floor and I on the fifth. James, the operator, did not stop at the third floor and went straight to the fifth. Dr. McCord asked why he missed his floor. He looked at President McCord and said, "Don't you know Dr. Gazes is on this elevator?" As I got off the elevator, I saluted President McCord.

Even though our medical school is one of the oldest in America, it did not become well-known until Dr. McCord became president. One of his greatest accomplishments was to end the strike that attempted to unionize the Medical University Hospital.

Dr. James Colbert was a very capable assistant for Dr. McCord as the first vice president of academic affairs. Unfortunately, he died in a 1974 plane crash and was survived by his wife and nine children. At the time of his death, Stephen Colbert was ten-years-old. Stephen is a satirist; at present is the host of television's *The Colbert Report*. Dr. Colbert and I often traveled with Dr. McCord to Columbia, SC, to meet with the state legislators.

Dr. Pratt-Thomas, one of the most beloved teachers at the Medical University, was president for two years. Dr. James Edwards, oral surgeon, former governor of South Carolina, and secretary of energy in President Reagan's cabinet, was president for seventeen years. Jim and I often exchanged stories. I told this one about him. *He was in a nursing home, and this elderly lady said, "I can tell you how old you are." He said, "No, you can't." She said, "Drop your pants." He did. She said, "Drop your shorts." He did. She said, "You are seventy-two-years-old." He said, "How did you know that?" She said, "You told me yesterday."*

Our current president is Dr. Ray Greenberg. He previously served several years as vice president. Dr. Greenberg is a very energetic young person who has led the Medical University to bigger status. At one time he appointed me to be grand marshal at the university graduation exercises. I had to wear a fancy cloak and hat, and carry a large heavy staff. The president asked me not to tell any of my stories. I had the cue to begin the graduation procession after the string music stopped. They apparently were not ready, and I told this story. *This lady died and went to heaven. St. Peter told her before she could enter she had to spell the word* love. *After a few months St. Peter called her to watch the gate because he had other business. The first person to come up was her husband. She said, "John, what happened?" He said, "After you died, I married this young girl and used your inheritance to buy a beautiful home in Miami. One day I was water skiing, hit the dock, and here I am." She said, "Before you can come in you have to spell a word. John said, "What is it?" She said, "Czechoslovakia."* President Greenberg got me back by having me give the opening prayer at a banquet. Naturally I could not tell a joke.

Dr. Edwin Boyle was an expert in blood lipids. He trained at Bethesda, came to Charleston, and started the Charleston Heart Study, which ran for many years. He was a very affable person who considered everyone a friend. On one occasion we were at a medical meeting at the Palmer House in Chicago. Walking down the hallway he met this person and stopped to talk with him. Finally, he called me over and said, "Come over, I want you to meet my close friend, Liberace, a famous flamboyant pianist." Liberace gave us his card to take to his manager and have a drink, and also get tickets to his program. I wanted to go see Jimmy Durante, but Edwin insisted that we go hear Liberace. This was a large dinner theater, and we were seated on the first floor near the stage. As soon as Liberace came out with his glitzy costume, he ran to our table, and hugged us and said, "Boys, we are going to have a great time tonight." Periodically during his program he came over to hug us.

Another time we were on an airplane coming back from a medical meeting in St. Louis. Edwin saw an individual sitting alone, and he mentioned that he was one of the physicians who gave a great talk at the meeting, so he went over to sit with him. The plane landed in Atlanta, and they went out and had a drink. Then the plane landed in Augusta, and they had another. Finally, we landed in Charleston. To Dr. Boyle's surprise, the man turned to Dr. Boyle and said, "Look, I am not a doctor. I am the movie actor McDonald Cary, and I play in the series Dr. Christian on TV." He came to Charleston to promote his series, and I don't think Edwin ever got over this. Edwin and I frequently exchanged stories.

A man was stopped by a state trooper for doing seventy in a fifty-mile-an-hour zone. "What is your excuse?" the trooper asked. The man said, "Officer, my wife ran away several months ago with a state trooper, and I thought you were bringing her back."

Senator Ernest Hollings and I have been friends since childhood. We went to elementary school and high school together but parted for college. He went to the Citadel and I to the College of Charleston. We have maintained our friendship and still periodically go out. Senator Strom Thurmond had been a patient for many years, and I usually saw him on a yearly basis. Once I was in Washington on a committee for the American College of Cardiology, and I visited him. When I went in his office I said, "Senator, there are many rumors about you in South Carolina. It's said that the DNA on Monica Lewinsky's dress is yours. He jumped up and said, "She is cute." His secretary almost fell out of her chair.

On a cold night on February 17, 1864, eight men squeezed through the small hatch of the *H.L. Hunley* in the harbor of Charleston, South Carolina. These eight men were the propulsion power for this revolutionary submarine. Hunley detonated a torpedo and blew up the U.S.S. *Housatonic*, a Union warship. Not long after, the *Housatonic* sank, and the *Hunley* also slipped to the bottom of the sea. In 1995, underwater archaeologists found the *Hunley*, and it was raised in August 2000. In January 2001, investigators went to work and carefully recovered the remains of the crew. The *Hunley* is now displayed at North Charleston. *The saying in Charleston is that when they went into the* Hunley *the first thing they found was a sign that read* Vote for Strom Thurmond for Senator. Thurmond was our oldest South Carolina senator and died at age 100. Many interesting stories have been told about him.

I would be remiss if I didn't mention several other friends, namely, Robert "Crusty" Rosemond, Waldo "Buck" Moore, Bruce Logue, Walker Bates, Milton Prystowsky, Ely Brooks, Walter Roberts, Clarence "Butch" Coker, Conyers O'Bryan, Nasseb B. Baroody, Pete "Budda" Pedersen, and Michael Gorman. We visited Crusty many times and stayed at his home in Sanford, Florida. I don't know how his lovely wife Sally has put up with him for so many years. He is an excellent doctor but likes to play tricks. One day he said I could pick oranges from trees across the street from his home. I assumed they were his. It was drizzling, and I put on a raincoat and proceeded up the ladder. In the meantime, Crusty called the neighbor who owned the trees and told him a poacher was in his orchard. Since this had happened before, the cantankerous old man came out with a shotgun. I almost fell from the ladder and had to do a lot of explaining.

Crusty, Tom Darby (whom I previously mentioned), and I were in Chicago and decided to go to Al Capone's old hideout at Ciceros. We went to the bar and an elderly lady (in her prime, a professional dancer) was dancing on the bar and stripping. This was not what we expected. Next to us at the bar were two young ladies drinking. When we went to pay, we discovered they had added their drinks to our bill. They were hired to do this and they were drinking tea. When we saw a huge bouncer coming our way, we paid the bill and got out quickly.

Buck was similar to Crusty. He lived in Atlanta with his lovely wife Nathalia. Athena and I often visited them for medical meetings and fun. Each morning at this home he would wake us by sending his dog Bobo into our room. Bobo would jump on the bed and lick our faces.

Bruce was a nationally known cardiologist. We often lectured together and co-authored medical articles. Once we wrote a chapter in Willis Hurst's textbook *The Heart* in the morning and played golf in the afternoon. What a surprise to see Bruce and his wife Caroline at a banquet in my honor. During that banquet, a kickoff for the cardiovascular research building that bears my name, Senator Fritz Hollings was the speaker. Other dignitaries made remarks including my good friend, Lieutenant Governor Nick Theodore.

Walker Bates, Ely Brooks, and Milton Prystowsky, my medical school classmates, often studied and had fun together. Walker and I shared a cadaver in our anatomy class. Ely entertained us with his stories. Milton studied with the only female in our class. One day I said, "You should get married," and they did.

Walter Roberts was one of my students who often called me Mister Doctor. One day as a staff physician he said, "You are really dressed well". I answered, "Look son, you can't hide looks and money." He often quoted this. He had a thriving practice in Columbia, South Carolina. When he was president of the South Carolina Medical Association at a banquet he presented me with the president's award.

Clarence "Butch" Coker, another student, practices family medicine in Manning, South Carolina. He had a small vegetable garden and agreed to plant some dandelions. Dandelions are weeds yet can also be beneficial to your health. A serving of dandelions contains 280 percent of an adult's daily requirement of beta-carotene as well as more than half of the requirement for vitamin C. They are also rich in vitamin A. Dandelions have a broad shaggy edge like teeth with deep roots and produce many tiny yellow flowers. The young leaves make an agreeable and wholesome addition to a salad. The older grown leaves are bitter. The young leaves are usually boiled. They are sprinkled with salt and pepper, and dribbled with lemon juice and olive oil. They are frequently eaten in France and Greece. Often many consume the liquid in which they are boiled. Butch called me one day to come and pick my dandelions. I was busy so he had them harvested and sent ten bushels to my home. Unfortunately, they were pulled up by their roots. Athena was beside herself. The dirt adhering to the roots had to be washed off and was a tedious, time-consuming procedure. The cleaned dandelions then were divided and packaged for freezing.

Butch and I were playing golf at the Waynesville Country Club in North Carolina. The eighth hole ran parallel to a street with homes on the other side. Butch, a very muscular person, drove his golf ball across the street and hit a doorbell at one of the homes. It was early in the morning, and a lady in her nightgown answered the door. She looked around but saw no one. Butch would not retrieve his golf ball. I often tell this story at medical meetings.

Conyers O'Bryan is a cardiologist in Florence, South Carolina. I taught him in medical school and also during his cardiac fellowship. He has been on our board of trustees for several years and served as chairman. I often ask for his support.

Naseeb B. Baroody is director of the cardiac clinic in the family practice program in Florence. He is an outstanding physician and photographer. His artwork is displayed on the clinic walls. These are also depicted in his book *In Search of His Image: A Photographic Journey.*

Pete "Buddha" Pederson, an attorney, often played golf in our group. He was called Buddha for he was stocky, muscular, had a potbelly, and was very much in charge. He was leader of our golf blitzes. He made up the teams. No one could play without his permission. He always told jokes and made arrogant remarks. One day after our blitz, I got up on a chair in the nineteenth hold bar and said, "Do any of your know why you can't circumcise an attorney?" There was no answer, so I said, "There is no end to the pricks (slang for penis). This time I got him. His wife's family has land on which tomatoes are grown. After they are commercially harvested, we are allowed to pick the remaining ripe tomatoes. Pete has lost weight, and his potbelly so we no longer call him the Buddha.

Michael Gorman, a pharmaceutical executive, has supported our annual Update Cardiology Seminar for over thirty years. It is amazing how he remembers so many names. He is acquainted with most cardiologists in American and elsewhere. He is often my golfing partner.

I have known Dr. Denton Cooley of Houston, Texas for many years. He is a well-recognized cardiac surgeon. He came to Charleston to speak just after he and Dr. Michael DeBakey had a dispute over a mechanical heart. At the night of the banquet, he was the speaker and I introduced him. *I said, "Dr. DeBakey was driving in Houston, and a policeman stopped him for speeding." He said, "Don't you know I am a very well-known cardiac surgeon?" The cop looked at him and said, "I don't care if you are Denton Cooley, I will give you a ticket."*

I became acquainted with Dr. DeBakey when we were on the Advisory Council for the National Heart Lung Blood Institute. He was a delightful, charming person, and very active for his age. One of our surgeons trained with him for a year and often mentioned how he could operate for several hours at a time.

Dr. DeBakey was seen by a car mechanic when he went to pick up his car. The mechanic said, "Hey, DeBakey come and see this." The famous surgeon was surprised but went over to where the mechanic was working. The mechanic said, "I also open hearts, take valves out, grind them, and put in new parts. So how come you get the big bucks when we basically are doing the same work?" Dr. DeBakey leaned over and whispered to the mechanic, "Have you tried doing it with the engine running?"

I have been very fortunate to have several wonderful secretaries who also became my friends. Beverly Clark worked in my outside private office. Cathy Martin, Peggy Wilder, and Linda Paddock were with me at the Medical University of South Carolina. It is impossible to describe all the work they have done. They were very loyal and dedicated.

Having a lovely family is very important. If families were closer, we would have fewer problems, especially with drugs. Parents should spend time and listen to their children. Friends are also very important for they contribute to a family.

Again through family and friends, I overcame many obstacles *through the back door.*

CHAPTER 9
AMERICA: OPPORTUNITY FOR ALL
Proud of My Country

America is the greatest country. Even though I had many obstacles and had to obtain my accomplishments *through the back door*, I could never have achieved them in another country. My immigrant parents came from Greece, made a great living, and had five children who were all educated. If you have motivation, persistence, and determination, you can accomplish everything you desire.

I traveled to many countries giving lectures and was always happy to return to the United States of America. Also, over a period of ten years, I visited many places traveling on cruise ships and lecturing. Many of the trips were associated with a cruise, and I had to give lectures only while at sea. Once the ship landed, my wife and I were free to tour. I would like to review a few of these trips.

In 1967, I went to Greece for six weeks as a visiting physician. This was my first trip to my parents' native land. Two weeks before leaving I went to get my passport. Unfortunately, I could not get it for I did not have a birth or baptism certificate. My sister Nicky, who kept these in a Bible, could not find them. I called the clerk of court in St. Matthews, South Carolina where I was born. They had no evidence of my birth since the old building had burned down. Next, I called vital statistics in Columbia, South Carolina, and they had no record. They sent me many forms to complete that would have been impossible in the time I had left. I remembered six months before this giving a lecture to the Orangeburg Medical Society. An elderly Dr. T.H. Symmes came to hear me from nearby St. Matthews. He mentioned he had delivered me. I called him and asked if he kept records of his deliveries. Fortunately, he did. He wrote an affidavit documenting my birth, and I received my passport just in time for the trip.

I visited many hospitals and gave many lectures in Greece. I also had time with my family to tour the country. Greece is a lovely land with its blue skies and blue waters. One of the famous sites in Greece is the Acropolis of Athens, which dates to the sixth century BC. The top is reached by a winding path, at the end of which stands the impressive gateway the Propylaea. The sacred way led to the Parthenon where once there was a great bronze statue of the goddess Athena. The other buildings on the Acropolis are the Erechtheum and Temple of Nike Apteros (Wingless Victory).

Below the Acropolis is the Odeum of Herodes Atticus with its theater. There we heard the famous pianist Van Clyburn give a recital with the king and queen in attendance. Clyburn played encores for one hour, since he was not allowed to leave before the king and queen stood up to depart. Greece no longer has a monarchy. Many treasures from the Acropolis are in the National Museum of Greece in Athens. The Elgin marbles, removed from the Parthenon, are in the British Museum in London. One of my favorite visits was to the Oracle at Delphi. Greeks asked advice from the oracles. The priestesses interpreted the oracles according to their whims. Greek men often get advice too—from their wives.

This man placed an advertisement in the newspaper to sell an encyclopedia. It was new and unused. Reason for sale: My wife knows everything.

In this area you could see excavation of statues coming out of the ground. Many of the heads were missing. Apparently this allowed them to be changed depending on the person's importance and political standing. Besides Athens we visited Sounion and the Temple of Apollo. We swam in the clear, cold water. We saw fish swimming down to the sandy bottom. A patient, a ship owner, arranged a cruise for our family to the Aegean Islands. The name of the ship was the *Argonaut.* It went from the port of Piraeus to Rhodes, Crete, Myconos, Delos, Santorini, and many other islands. Crete had one of the world's earliest civilizations (Minoan). The remains of the Minoan palace at Knossos were amazing. Clay pipes could be seen that were used for their drainage system dating back to 1100 BC. Santorini, thought by some to be lost Atlantis, could only be reached by a motor launch from the cruise ship. We went by donkey to the top of the island. A lift is now available. This was exciting and very treacherous, for the donkey would wander along the edge of the path going up, and you could see the precipitous side of the mountain of rocks down to the sea. There were no rails, and you feared that the donkey would throw you over the cliff. Fortunately, I speak Greek; otherwise the donkey would not have understood me.

Kos in the Aegean Sea is the second largest island in the Dodecanese. It was an important cultural center, and the home of the physician Hippocrates, recognized as the father of medicine. The Hippocratic oath represents his own ideals. His writings contain aphorisms, the airs, waters, and places. We saw the Hippocratic museum nearby the plane tree under the shade of which he supposedly taught. The plane tree of 500 years is a distant offshoot of the original tree. Asklepeion, erected during the third century BC, a renowned treatment center, was built on a hill with the town of Kos and its suburbs spreading at its base. The physicians of the Asklepeion (who also were priests) had adopted the Hippocratic method of diagnosis and treatment. Their symbol was a snake because of its ability to discover therapeutic herbs. The Asklepeion originally consisted of a religious sanctuary, healing centre, school of medicine, and many mineral springs where people went to bathe. It has three terraces linked together with short staircases. At night in downtown Kos, we were entertained by modern dancing and singing.

Rhodes is the largest Dodecanese island in the Aegean. It belongs to Greece. At the entrance to its ancient harbor stood the Colossus of Rhodes, one of the Seven Wonders of the World. The Colossus is thought to have been a huge bronze statue of Apollo. It was built between 292-280 BC with a height of 106 feet. There are many stories about it. One suggests that the legs of the statue straddled the harbor entrance. About 226 BC, an earthquake destroyed it. Nothing of it remains today. The arts and sciences flourished in Rhodes, and it became the seat of a famous school of rhetoric. Julius Caesar studied there. Many Germans visit Rhodes in August and swim at their beaches. It has become known as the Miami of Germany. Lindos in Rhodes, one of the three ancient states of Rhodes, has a maze of narrow cobbled streets and whitewashed houses that cling to the hillside that is topped by an acropolis. The acropolis was excavated between 1902 and 1912. Tools dating back to 3000 BC were found. You can go up to the acropolis by donkey or by the monumental staircase, which is a good stress test. The way down by donkey may be treacherous since they race down to get food and water. The walk surrounding the acropolis gives a sense of the medieval. A beautiful site in Rhodes is the Valley of the Butterflies. From June to September there are countless numbers of them.

Many of the doctors in Greece have been trained in America. In 1967, they did not have the proper equipment. However, over the years they have become very competitive. The Hellenic Congress of Cardiology had an international meeting, and I was fortunate to be invited as a cardiologist from America. A Greek doctor friend told me to speak only in English, even though I can speak Greek. Behind the podium there were many small rooms with interpreters. The audience could use their earphones and listen in any language they desired. After my talk they all clapped, but I did not leave the podium. Instead, I thanked them in Greek for having me since my parents were from Greece. They didn't realize I could speak Greek and gave me a standing ovation.

Dr. Samaras, head cardiologist at the Evangelismon Hospital, and his wife, Lena, took Athena and me for dinner at the Queen's Club in Athens. Lena's family gave the famous Bonanki Museum to Athens. This was a very large family home that now houses the museum and has a wonderful restaurant at the top level. The Samaras have two sons. One became an architect and the other, Antonios, went into politics. He is now a member of the Greek parliament. In July 1967, I saw him as patient at his home. He had developed a form of heart block with a slow heart rate. He had planned to go in September to Amherst College in Boston. Dr. Samaras called a famous cardiologist in the United States and was told not to send him because of his son's condition. I noticed that he had infectious mononucleosis, which may cause a heart block. This usually clears, and when it did, he was able to attend Amherst, where he received a degree in economics. In 1976, he received a MBA from Harvard. Before dinner, Dr. Samaras poured a glass of ouzo and drank it down quickly. Since it didn't seem to bother him I drank my glass down quickly. I broke out in a cold sweat and felt miserable. A kitchen was nearby, and I ran in and ate some squid, trying to neutralize the ouzo. Ouzo on ice or with water turns milky white, and I now call it Greek white lightning."

I made rounds with Dr. Samaras and his medical staff, and spoke at the Evangelismon Hospital. The lecture room was on the top floor and had a large glass window. I had a peculiar sensation lecturing and seeing the Acropolis such a short distance away. No building in Greece can be higher than the Acropolis.

My parents came from the Ionian side of Greece and Athena's from the Aegean side. On our first visit in 1967, I met two of my maternal uncles and several paternal cousins. Since my parents never returned to Greece, they were delighted that they could see and entertain us. Athena's paternal uncle,

Louis, was a character. He was an active ninety-year-old. He went to a well and pulled out a bottle of ouzo. I thought he was going for cold water. It was 10:00 in the morning and very hot. He began Greek dancing and drinking ouzo. He invited me to do the same. By noon I could not see. His wife cooked in an outside oven. Her baked bread and lamb chops were wonderful.

My last trip to Greece was during the terrorist attack on America on 9/11. We had just returned from a seven-day cruise in the Aegean. A friend of ours who knew a wealthy person was able to obtain his 162-foot yacht, which was motorized and had sails. The owner paid over $25 million to have it built. There were eight of us, and eight crew members, including a chef. Each morning we were asked by the captain which island we would like to visit. Since we had previously seen the touristy islands of Mykonos, Rhodes, Crete, and others we went to islands infrequently visited. We visited the Saronics (Hydra, Spetses, Aegina, and Poros), and Nafplion, a seaport town in the Peloponnese. No cars are allowed on Hydra, and we had to visit an ancient church by donkey. Spetses is known for its annual Amata Festival celebrating the naval battle of the 1821 revolution. Bouboulina, a female admiral, led this battle against the Turks. We happened to be there during this annual celebration. There was a dramatization of the victory performed at night. Real ships were used and a model Turkish flagship was built especially for the occasion. The ship was burned, and at the same time there was a huge display of fireworks. After our cruise ended, we returned to Athens and saw on TV the news about 9/11. Getting back home was impossible, since all flights were canceled. After a week we were able to book a flight back to America. We have had at least twenty visits to Greece. All have been very enjoyable.

Before the Berlin Wall came down, we visited East Berlin. After two hours at Checkpoint Charlie in extremely cold weather, guarded by machine guns, we were allowed to go through. In addition, they took our passports. East Berlin was very gloomy. It seemed that everyone was sad, and there were no children playing. We toured one of their hospitals. It was very out of date. One of their physicians said they cured people quite differently than we do in America. He showed us a large room where patients were treated with mud baths. Only their heads were visible. The rest of the bodies were covered by mud. The site of all in East Berlin was the Pergamon Museum. It has many relics taken from Greece. The great alter of Pergamon is a massive work of sculpture originally built in the second century in the ancient city of Pergamon. It has a long frieze depicting the struggle of the gods and giants. My wife and I were walking down the street when we saw an Orthodox Christian Church.

We entered and there were many old people. The church did not have any pews. The entire liturgy was in German. It was obvious that the priest was Greek. Afterwards we approached and asked why his sermon was in German. He said it was in the language of the country. On leaving East Berlin, we were again detained for two hours at the wall. They searched every little nook on the bus to see if anyone was hiding to escape to the West.

Budapest occupies both banks of the river Danube. It was formed by unification of the right bank Buda with the left bank Pest. Buda is rather hilly. Pest lies on flat terrain.

On our trip to Budapest, a couple we met invited us to go to a restaurant with a friend of theirs who worked in Budapest. This friend had heard of a great restaurant on the Buda side. After an hour in a taxi we were in a very dark area with what appeared to be a vacant filling station. Inside was a restaurant filled with many strange people. Instead of the violins we expected, there was a brass band playing American songs. The tables were dirty and the food was terrible. A couple from another table, who could not speak English, grabbed my wife and me to dance. The woman I danced with weighed about 200 pounds, and she lifted me off the floor. Later she returned to dance again, and I told her with a motion of my hand that my heart was beating irregularly. A tall man in a red outfit asked my wife to dance. She refused, and all night long he sat at the next table shaking his fist at me. Another man came over to sell us cocaine, which he had in a matchbox. We refused, and he became upset. By this time we felt sure we would be robbed and perhaps never leave the restaurant alive. Fortunately, one member of our party had told the cab driver to return. When he came, we all followed him out, and we were not attacked. It appeared that a trick was played on the lady who recommended this place. A friend of hers said it was an outstanding restaurant not realizing she was taking two other couples with her.

The next day we went to Vienna on the river Danube by hydrofoil. It skimmed the water and traveled very fast. To complete my lectures, I had to give one on the hydrofoil. The noise was so intense I had to wander between the physicians so that they could hear me.

One of the major tourist attractions in Vienna is the world's oldest zoo. It houses giant pandas, lions, tigers, and many other animals. We happened to visit the zoo while they were feeding. What a gruesome ordeal this was! At Vienna I made up for the fiasco at Budapest by taking my wife to a very fancy restaurant with great food and violins.

Salzburg, Austria, is one of the most beautiful cities in Europe. There is nothing better than sipping apple schnapps while listening to the music of Mozart. *The Sound of Music* was filmed at a castle in Salzburg. The castle is striking with its beautiful gazebo.

General Mark Clark was a great friend and patient of mine. At the close of World War II he became the American Occupation Commander in Austria. Eisenhower had the same job in Germany. General Clark was a distinguished, clever intellectual and ranks with Eisenhower, Patton, Bradley, MacArthur, and Nimitz as the greatest of American leaders who brought victory in World War II. General Patton, after he slapped a soldier, was assigned to General Clark. They dined together, and one night General Patton got up to go to bed early. Clark asked him why so early. Patton said, "I am going to pray that the enemy beats you, so I can get my command back."

I mentioned to General Clark that we had visited Berchtesgaden and saw Hitler's bunkers and the Eagle's Nest on the top of a high mountain. After the close of World War II, General Clark obtained some souvenirs from the Eagle's Nest. When I told him of our visit, he went to his safe and gave me a spoon from Hitler's collection, which bears a Swastika insignia. I have the spoon and a note from General Clark mounted in my study. General Clark lived several doors down from me and often he would visit, have a drink, and tell me many interesting stories. In 1944, when General Clark and the Fifth Army captured Rome, he was in a jeep surrounded by soldiers. A priest on a bicycle came up and said that Pope Pius XII wanted to see him. The general said he would go, provided the pope blessed his Catholic troops. In 1975, the Fifth Army had a reunion in Rome and he met with Pope Paul VI. The pope asked, "Do you recognize me?" The general was puzzled. "I was the priest on the bicycle who came to you when Rome was liberated." General Clark gave me a picture of Pope Paul VI shaking his hand, and he autographed it, "To Athena and Pete, from the two old Roman Ruins."

When I first saw the general as a patient he was very active in many projects. I told him he had to slow down for a while and give no more speeches.

The AOA is our Medical Honor Society for students who rank at the top of their class. Each year they have a black tie banquet and invite a well-known speaker. A few days before the banquet, the president of the AOA called and said their speaker was sick. I was their counselor. I thought for a few minutes and then I called on General Clark to speak. He graciously accepted. During cocktail hour, he asked me what he should talk about. Since General Patton was assigned to him for a year I thought he should speak of their association. General Clark began his speech by saying, "I certainly have a wonderful doctor. After advising me to give no speeches, he calls me a week later asking that I give this talk." I almost sank under the table. For one hour he kept the audience mesmerized. Speaking to the medical professions can be very difficult, but for the general it was a breeze.

I often saw General Clark on Sunday mornings before church. During one visit he had a phone call from President Reagan. When he was stationed on the West Coast, Clark's daughter told him she was to have a date with a movie star. The general was against this. It turned out the date was Ronald Reagan, and the general and Reagan became great friends. General Clark was appointed chairman of the American Battle Monuments Commission, and he held this post from 1969 until his death in 1984. Athena and I visited Anzio Beach and the Memorial Garden at Nettuno. General Clark had a Colonel Brown, who was in charge of the Garden show us around. First we visited Anzio Beach where Clark's Fifth Army landed. Anzio was an important step on the way to capturing Rome. During the battle 36,000 men died. Colonel Brown said the water at the beach turned red from blood. The Benedictine Abbey at the top of Monte Cassino dominated the approach to Anzio. General Clark was against bombing the abbey. The British decided to go ahead anyway, and they demolished the monastery. Clark had counterintelligence agents investigate and they discovered there were no Germans there.

At Nettuno there was a memorial building with an atrium at the entrance with marble columns forming a circle. In the middle there was a granite pedestal topped by a bronze sculpture of two American military personnel (Brothers in Arms). The cemetery was immaculate. The graves of 7,000 American soldiers were marked by long rows of white crosses.

On a Sunday, June 1, 1980, Athena and I received a call from General Clark to come over and have a drink since it was our anniversary. We had a great surprise in store, for Delores Hope was his guest. Bob Hope was to come later. Athena and Delores had a long conversation about grandchildren. Delores sang the anniversary song for us. General Clark frequently had very important guests at his home whom we met.

Once in New York, in civilian clothes, General Clark took a cab. The driver said, "You look like Mark Clark." Clark answered, "I wish I did." The driver made an illegal turn and was stopped by a policeman. The driver said, "That's Mark Clark in the backseat, and he is in a hurry." The policeman looked inside, saluted, and then waved the taxi on. The driver chuckled, "We sure fooled him." General Clark always enjoyed such stories, and he told me this one.

There was a big muscular student walking around the Citadel Campus where General Clark was president after he retired from the army. The football coach asked this student if he could pass a football, and he said, "Yee gads, if I can eat it, I can pass it.

Athena and I have made several trips with our patriarch, the head of the Orthodox Christian Church. This was indeed an honor, and we were able to visit many interesting places. Once, we spent a week in Rome, where the patriarch celebrated mass with Pope John Paul II. Afterward, a reception was held at the Vatican, and we were able to speak to the pope. He was a very humble and warm person who radiated with spirituality. He smiled and blessed the rosaries, which I had brought for my Catholic friends, and next my wife went up to him. She was so taken aback that she could not speak. The pope noticed the rosaries, blessed them, and she went on. The pope visited with our patriarch several times, for it was their hope that in the future the Orthodox Christian Church will celebrate communion with the Roman Catholic Church. Before 1054 they were one church. We also visited Venice with the patriarch. This is another beautiful city, with all its canals and the Piazzo San Marco. Taking a gondola and listening to Italian singers was really a treat. There was a beautiful Orthodox Church in Venice. Its priest, who was born in America, subsequently became the American archbishop.

The pope came to America and took a cab to the United Nations. He told the cab driver to get there in a hurry. The driver said, "Your holiness, I have two tickets already. If I get another one, they will take away my license." The pope said, "You sit in the backseat, and I will drive." The pope was stopped for speeding, and the policeman said, "Wait here, your holiness." He called his dispatcher and said, "I have a VIP and don't know what to do." The dispatcher said, "Who is he?" The policeman said, "I don't know, but the pope is his chauffer."

While in Rome we saw many important sites. At St. Peter's Basilica we saw Michelangelo's Pieta, sculpted from a single piece of marble when Michelangelo was only twenty-three. A short time before our visit, a deranged artist had defaced the sculpture. It was restored and now is kept behind plate glass. We also saw the marble sculpture of Moses in the Minor Church of San Pietro in Vincole Church in Rome, which originally was intended for the tomb of Julius II in St. Peter's Basilica. The statue depicts Moses with horns on his head. The horns are there because of a mistranslation from the Hebrew, where the word *karen* may mean either radiated light or grew horns. The Moses sculpture is one of Michelangelo's greatest masterpieces. The statue's eyes seem to follow you wherever you go in the room. His fingers can be seen winding through his long beard. The marble appears soft without giving up any of the strength and majesty that his pieces possess. His facial features, swollen veins on his left arm, and muscles are very real.

The Sistine Chapel is the best-known chapel in the world. Between 1508 and 1512, under the patronage of Pope Julius II, Michelangelo painted the 12,000-square-foot ceiling. Even though he disliked the commission, it is widely thought to be his crowning achievement. Today the chapel serves as the place for the ceremony of selecting a new pope. The ceiling has a series of nine paintings showing God's creation of the world, God' relationship with mankind, and mankind's fall from God's grace. Michelangelo later painted a depiction of the Last Judgment on the wall behind the altar. The pictorial program for the chapel shows scenes from the New and Old Testaments about the lives of Christ and Moses. The Sistine Chapel's ceiling was restored in 1984. I was fortunate to see it before and after the restoration. Some think the work was overdone because the colors are now so bright. Michelangelo's work includes a self-portrait of himself as St. Bartholomew, after the saint was flayed (skinned alive). It reflects the painter's contempt for being commissioned to paint the Last Judgment. The painting on the ceiling of the Sistine Chapel is a detailed depiction of some of Christianity's and Judaism's most famous moments. The ceiling is almost eighty-four feet above ground. When I looked up at it, the arms and legs of many of the figures seemed to be dangling from the ceiling.

This a letter an Italian man wrote to Sears Roebuck. My brother Pat often recited it.

Dear Mr. Robuca,

I have a complaint. My wife came to your store and bought a ten-cent can of paint. She likes to keep our home clean and neat, so she painted the toilet seat. My sister Marie—she came to live with us—sat down and got paint on her all around. I ran to the store and got turpentine, and I rubbed so hard she almost lost her mind. I rubbed all day, and the skin came off but the paint she stay. Now Mr. Robuca, this is my complaint. How can my wife keep her home clean and neat if the paint won't dry on the toilet seat?

Jerusalem is located in the Judean Mountains (Mount of Olives and Mount Scopus) between the Mediterranean Sea and the northern tip of the Dead

Sea. Modern Jerusalem has grown beyond the boundaries of the old city. The old walled city has been traditionally divided into four quarters, the Armenian, Christian, Jewish, and Muslim. The Wailing or Western Wall is the remains of the great Jewish temple destroyed by the Romans. The Wailing Wall is a holy place of the Jews. It is visited by millions of worshipers. Prayers are offered and notes containing many wishes are wedged between the crevices. In the Christian quarter is the Church of the Holy Sepulcher. This was the site of the Crucifixion, and the tomb where the body of Christ was laid. We had an opportunity to see it with our patriarch one night, on a special visit without the daytime mobs. Through this quarter runs the Via Dolorosa, where Jesus is said to have carried his cross. Outside the old city are the Garden of Gethsemane and the Mount of Olives in which Christ taught his disciples the Lord's Prayer.

Cana is where Jesus performed his first miracle by turning water into wine. On our visit there we renewed our marriage vows. I asked the priest if we could also renew our honeymoon. He only laughed.

The beatitudes were eight blessings uttered by Jesus at the opening of the Sermon on the Mount. A church is built over the Mount with a superb view of the lake and the beatitudes were inscribed in a circle on the building. We also went to the Jordan River with our patriarch and renewed our baptismal vows.

In 1954 I went to Cuba to lecture. A lady who had a popular Italian restaurant in Charleston was gong to visit there since she had bought some property on an island near Cuba. We went with her, her husband, and a Catholic priest. We drove to Miami and stayed at this lady's brother's hotel. The hotel was not first class, but it was adequate. The next morning the priest said that he saw many women entering and leaving the hotel. A midget was standing by and said, "You didn't know this is a whorehouse, and that I am the pimp?"

The Charleston lady had not visited her brother for many years and did not realize that he was in so many odd activities. At that time, Batista was in power in Cuba. There were only two classes of people, the very rich and the very poor. It was pathetic to watch young children begging in the streets. The Isle of Pines (Isla de Pinos) nearby was where our friend had her property. In 1978, its name has been changed to Isla de la Juventud. There was a model prison there. One man from a central station could operate all of the cells. The prisoners prepared all of their food and made many objects, including marble bookends (I have a set). These were sold, and the prisoners could keep some of the income. For good behavior, they could stay on weekends with their families in small cottages near the prison. Fidel Castro was imprisoned there from 1953 to 1955. After the revolution the facility was used to imprison political enemies of Castro. This now serves as a museum and is declared a national monument. Among other things in Cuba, adultery and thievery were serious problems.

Many jokes begin in prison. At night all the prisoners congregate in the so-called bull pen. A new prisoner came in and heard prisoners giving out numbers and laughing. He asked what goes on. An old prisoner said, "We have heard the jokes so often we give them number.s" He said, "Twenty-four," and everyone laughed. The new prisoner said, "Can I say one? Ten." Nobody laughed. The old prisoner said, "Look, it is not the joke, it is how you tell it."

This young man went to confess adultery. The priest said, "With whom?" The young man said, "I can't tell you." The priest said, "Is it Mary Brown, Louise John, or Mary Smith?" The young man said, "I can't tell you." The priest said, "Then I cannot give you absolution." On the way home the young man saw a friend and told him, "I met a wonderful priest. I went to confess adultery, and he gave me three new names."

A priest was reciting the Ten Commandments. When he said thou shall not steal, he saw that a parishioner was anxious. When he said thou shall not commit adultery, the parishioner was smiling. After the service, the priest asked the parishioner what his problem was. The parishioner answered, "When you said thou shall not steal, I noticed my umbrella was missing. And when you said thou shall not commit adultery, I remembered where I left it."

The Cha-Cha-Cha dance had just come in vogue when we saw Cab Calloway performing it. I learned the dance in Cuba and I am still able to do this. Cuba had great entertainment. The Flamingo was a popular nightclub. The singing and dancing were superb. Many of the entertainers could not come to America, and, their income was so small that during the day they worked in various stores to make extra money.

We made several trips to London. London is a remarkable city with its famous cabs and courteous drivers. The Tower of London and Tower Bridge, Big Ben, Saint Paul's Cathedral, the British Museum, Westminster Abbey, and the antique malls are just a few of its important sites. Athena and I went to a pub to eat shepherd's pie. It's a layer of mashed potatoes with ground beef in between. It was delicious until I made the comment, "I wonder if this is horse meat?"

On my first visit I made patient rounds at the old Guy's hospital. Many cardiac patients were kept in an open ward by their socialized medical system.

Many required surgery but often had to wait for a year. While waiting, some of the patients would die unless they offered to pay a private doctor for the procedure. I visited the National Heart Hospital. Much excellent research came out of this hospital, even though it was very small and had very simple equipment. The English could perform many research projects with little equipment. This hospital has been closed for the past several years. After visiting London, we went to Oxford and Stratford-on-Avon. Stratford-on-Avon is a market town and civil parish in South Warwickshire, England, and lies on the River Avon. The town is a popular tourist destination since it is the birthplace of William Shakespeare. The Royal Shakespeare Theatre was completed in 1932 and is the home of the Royal Shakespeare Company. The town includes five homes related to Shakespeare's life. Near the town is Anne Hathaway's cottage, the home of Shakespeare's wife before her marriage.

To the north of England lies Scotland. Edinburgh is its capital and a very interesting city. At our medical banquet we had a traditional Scottish dish called haggis. Sheep's heart, liver, and lungs are minced with onions, oatmeal, suet, spices, and salt. This is mixed with stock and traditionally boiled in sheep's stomach for approximately three hours. It resembles the Greek dish Kokoretsi, which I ate in Greece. At first I was reluctant to eat haggis, for from its description it did not seem appetizing. The sheep's stomach was brought to our table, cut open, and its contents placed on our plate. After sampling its excellent nutty texture and delicious, savory flavor, I ate it all. I had hoped to play one of Scotland's famous golf courses at St. Andrews, but unfortunately I was too involved in medical meetings.

This man had just joined a golf course, and by mistake, he went into the ladies shower room. He realized this when he heard female voices. Not avoid being recognized, he covered his head with a towel and ran out. Three ladies watched him and one said, "That's not my husband." The second one said, "He is not my husband." The third lady said, "Why, he isn't even a member of the club."

A man asked his priest if there is a golf course in heaven. The priest said, "I don't know, but I will find out." After several days the priest saw the man and said, "Yes, there is a beautiful golf course in heaven. Your tee time is 9:00 A.M. tomorrow."

Paris is another beautiful European city. It is frightening how fast people drive their cars there. They have no posted speed limit. We saw the usual touristy things, such as the Eiffel Tower, but what stood out the greatest for us was the Notre Dame Cathedral. This magnificent gothic structure, with its rose-colored windows of stained glass, its ornate spires, and gargoyles is very impressive. Victor Hugo's famous novel *The Hunchback of Notre Dame* made many aware of this wonderful cathedral. After entering its massive doors, you are taken by its famous stained glass windows. There are many sculptures in the deeply recessed niches of the cathedral.

The hunchback of Notre Dame, Quasimodo, was ringing the bell in the Tower of Notre Dame Cathedral. He grew tired and asked a derelict alcoholic to help him. He instructed the alcoholic to first pull the rope and ring the bell, and when the bell came back to hit it with his head. The alcoholic man did so, but the bell hit his face, and he fell off the tower into the square. People gathered around, for they didn't know who the man was. They looked up and said, "Perhaps Quasimodo knows." Quasimodo came down from the tower, looked at the man, and said, "I don't know who he is, but his face sure rings a bell."

A friend of ours in Paris who had a perfume shop took us one day to Marseilles. It is the second largest city in France and its chief Mediterranean port. From the sea it is a gleaming white city rising on a semicircle of hills. We went to a restaurant that served a delicious dessert called baba rhum. This was a sweet cake soaked in rum. It originally came from Poland where the dry Kugelhopf cake was dipped in rum to make baba. It was named after the character Ali Baba from the *One Thousand and One Nights*. This is the first time I got drunk from eating a dessert.

Asian Turkey is separated from European Turkey by the Bosporus, the Sea of Marmara and the Dardanelles (which link the Black Sea and the Mediterranean). These seas, the Aegean West, Black Sea North, and the Mediterranean South, encircle Turkey. At one time, many Greeks lived in Turkey. The number has dwindled. Our patriarch still remains in Turkey in a very small part of Istanbul that the Turks control. The famous Hagia Sophia was once a Christian church and the seat of Orthodoxy. It was taken over by the Turks and converted into a mosque. Its magnificent icons and mosaics were plastered over. Hagia Sophia is now a museum. Restoration has been going on for years. Orthodox Christians are not permitted by the Turks to celebrate liturgy at Hagia Sophia.

Saint John Chrysostom in the year 398 took the position of Greek Archbishop of Constantinople. He is known for the Divine Liturgy of Saint John Chrysostom or celebration of the Holy Eucharist. To this day Eastern Orthodox and most Eastern Catholic churches celebrate this liturgy. He died in exile in the city of Comana, Turkey, in the year 407. After thirty years, his relics were transferred to Constantinople. The relics were looted from Constantinople by the Crusaders in 1204 and brought to Rome. The late Pope John Paul II in the year 2004 consigned part of the relics to the Ecumenical Orthodox Patriarch

Bartholomew of Constantinople. Saint John Chrysostom's silver and jewel-encrusted skull is now kept in a monastery on Mount Athos, in northern Greece.

Halki, a beautiful Greek theological school on a mountain, was closed by the Turks but attempts are now being made to restore this to an active school. We were driven there by a horse-drawn buggy.

Machu Picchu was a famous fortress of the ancient Incas in what is now Peru. It was impossible to believe that such a fortress could have been built at the high altitude of 7,875 feet above sea level. There is a winding road from Cuzco to Machu Picchu. We were driven there in a small bus. The road is so narrow that it accommodates just one vehicle at a time. At turns there are wider areas where cars back up so other vehicles can pass. This was indeed frightening.

On a foggy night a man was following a car that suddenly stopped. Enraged, he said, "Why didn't you signal to stop?" The driver said, "Why should I? I am in my own garage."

Cuzco is a small village that one time was the capital of the Incan Empire. The day we arrived, it was very cold, and the hotel had only small heaters that worked very poorly. Because of the altitude, we all developed headaches. I took several medications. These gave me very little relief. In addition, I had to sleep with my hat and overcoat on because it was so cold. The next day, before going to Machu Picchu, we took a train, which zigzagged around the mountain. By the time we descended a few thousand feet, my headache cleared, but I was still a zombie from the medication. I looked out the train window and saw a lady wearing a long gown. She was squatting. She looked at me and smiled. When she got up there was a puddle of urine. Such were the doings in Peru.

We visited the so-called vacation cities of Russia, Yalta and Odessa. These were very depressing. The people did not appear happy and there were no children playing. We visited a museum in Yalta. It had poor lighting and displayed small, broken relics from other countries. In 1945, the Yalta Conference between the Soviet Union, the United States, and the United Kingdom was held.

In 1991, after the collapse of communism, Odessa became a part of the newly independent Ukraine. It is known for its huge outdoor market, the biggest of its kind in Europe. Other attractions include the catacombs, beaches, open theater, and the giant Potemkin stairs.

During our visit there we learned that Hurricane Hugo had hit Charleston. It took at least four days to get home. Fortunately, we had little damage, and our children had our home secure.

We have traveled to Bermuda, Mexico, and many cities in the United States. One interesting trip was to Bozeman, Montana. One morning I had to lecture at 7:00 A.M. in an auditorium across from our lodge. The temperature was minus fifty degrees Fahrenheit. On arrival at the auditorium, I could not speak until I sat before a fireplace and had some brandy. It was so cold that snow skiing was impossible.

We took a snowmobile to the Grand Canyon. The trees were laden with ice and snow. We saw many animals running in the snow. I also lectured at Jackson Hole, Wyoming, a gateway to the nearby Grand Teton National Park, Yellowstone National Park, and the National Elk Refuge. The Teton Mountain range is a dramatic view from Jackson Hole. The Cathedral groups of the Tetons are classic alpine peaks caused by glacial motion. Grand Teton means *large teat.* Teat is an alternative word for nipples of the breast. Tit is the Old English for teat and in modern English, slang for breast.

A boss told a young woman he would have to terminate her job because her breasts were so prominent men in the office lost time by looking at her. She said, "That's no problem." She had falsies and threw them in the trashcan. The boss went over to the trashcan and threw in his false teeth and said, "Bite them, you always wanted to."

Bermuda is a British territory in the Atlantic Ocean. From Charleston it is almost a direct route to Bermuda, which lies due east of Fripp Island, South Carolina. Although it is often referred to as a single island, the territory consists of many small islands. The city of Hamilton is its capital. During the American War of 1812, the British attacks on Washington, DC, and the Chesapeake were planned and launched from Bermuda. This war inspired the writing of "The Star-Spangled Banner." Bermuda has become a popular destination for tourists, 80 percent of whom are from the United States. Cruise ships often sail from Charleston to Bermuda. In 1974, 100 doctors and their wives chartered a plane from Charleston to Bermuda for a medical meeting. Four of us from the Medical University went. The people were very pleasant, and the food was superb. Many enjoyed traveling by scooter over islands roads. Unfortunately there were some accidents.

Acapulco is a city and major seaport on the Pacific coast of Mexico. It is a popular resort for tourists from the United States. The beaches are very popular, and the glass-bottom motorboats give a clear view of the bottom of the sea. The Acapulco Cliff divers are featured regularly and seen on ABC's Wide World of Sports. After our morning medical meeting, several of us went to play golf. On returning to our hotel, we saw our very popular pathologist teacher drinking with the ladies. We had a drink, too, and one doctor insisted on paying the bill for our pathologist professor. This opened the generous doctor's eyes, for the bill was over $600. The professor and ladies had been drinking all morning. I escaped paying *through the back door*.

Speaking about islands, this is a story I heard—

A man was shipwrecked and the lone survivor on an island. After several years there was another shipwreck and only one woman survived. She looked at him and said, "I know you crave a cigarette," and she unzipped a pocket and gave him a pack of Camels. Next she said, "I know that you would love a drink." She unzipped another pocket and gave him a bottle of Scotch. Next she said, "I know that you would like to play around." She began to unzip her blouse. He said, "I can't believe you also have golf clubs.

Other places I have lectured were in Australia, Puerto Rico, and Alaska. Australia was a very long airplane trip. The country reminded me of America fifty years ago. Sydney and Melbourne are two of their main cities. The convention center at Sydney is an architectural gem. There are many distinctive forms of animal life in Australia, including the kangaroo.

On our cruise ship there was a retired golf pro, hired by the ship to give lessons. We became friends and played the Royal Melbourne golf course together. This is the most prestigious, exclusive, and oldest golf club in Australia.

Puerto Rico is a United States territory. Its capital is San Juan. I was on a program for the Puerto Rican Heart Association. We were housed at the luxurious El Dorado Beach Hotel. The morning of the meeting I went over early to the auditorium. No one was there. I asked at the desk and was told the meeting would start at 9:00 A.M. I waited until 9:00, and no one came. I went back to the desk and the lady said, "Apparently you are not aware of Puerto Rican time." The meeting began at 9:30, and there at least 500 doctors showed up. I told the moderator that I could shorten my talk, but he didn't agree. The meeting ended about two hours over time. Drs. Enrique Pijem, Etienne Otaño, and Salomon Monserrate are great friends. There are many sites in Puerto Rico as the Fort San Felipe del Morro and the city walls. Old San Juan is a beautiful area and has the best pina coladas. The tropical rain forest has 240 species of trees, many waterfalls and is the home of fifty bird species. The Puerto Rican parrot is a rare and endangered species.

A husband bought his wife a parrot that could speak several languages for her birthday. He came home and asked his wife, "Did you get the bird?" She said, "Yes, he is in the oven." The husband said, "That bird could speak several languages." Wife, "Then, why didn't he say something?"

One of our best cruises was to Alaska; the ship docked at many places— Juneau, Sitka, Ketchikan, Skagway, and Anchorage. We stayed overnight at the foot of Mount McKinley. The mountain is the highest point in North America and is called Denali by the Indians. We went part of the way by bus; the snow was beautiful. On return we went by train to Fairbanks. Russia is not far away, and at one time, it owned Alaska. The United States bought it in 1867 for $7,200,000. Gold was discovered there, which made it a thriving area. One of the economic mainstays for the people is the Alaskan salmon. The Trans-Alaskan pipeline is one of the largest pipeline systems in the world, and the only way to get crude oil from Alaska's North Slope to tankers. This pipeline annually transports twenty five percent of U.S. oil production.

Our last night in Alaska we ate large oysters. The first one I ate tasted funny. That night I had severe diarrhea. We had to get up at 5:00 A.M. to catch a plane to Seattle. Thank the Lord for Lomotil. The diarrhea stopped just before I got on the plane.

After visiting many countries, I realized that America is the greatest. I thank God every day for having my parents settle here. Only in America could a young Greek of immigrant parents become a doctor and achieve so many things. I had to overcome many trials and tribulations *through the back door*, but it was worth it to be an American.

CHAPTER 10
REFLECTIONS
Medicine at the Crossroads

I have observed the development of diagnostic studies and therapy for cardiovascular diseases since 1950. No one could ever imagine the changes that have occurred. It started before 1950 with the electrocardiogram devised by Einthoven. He used the first string galvanometer to record the electrical activities of the heart. He described various irregularities and abnormalities. In 1948, the National Heart Institute established the Framingham Heart Study, which focused on prevention. Cholesterol, one of the risk factors for coronary heart disease was extensively studied. From 1940 to 1950, the two-step ECG stress test was developed by Dr. Masters. During that time X-rays of the heart and cardiac fluoroscopy were often used. From 1950 to 1960, Wolferth and Wilson developed the twelve-lead electrocardiogram. When I returned to Charleston in 1950, they were performing only four-lead electrocardiograms and consequently were missing many abnormalities. After several lectures I gave at the medical school, they would not accept this, and I had to develop the first twelve-lead electrocardiogram at St. Francis Hospital, *through the back door.* In 1929, Forssman performed right heart catheterization on himself by passing a catheter through a vein under fluoroscopic guidance into the right chambers of his heart. This was expanded by Andre Cournand and Dickinson Richards, who recorded intracardiac pressures and cardiac output (quantity of blood pumped by the heart into the aorta per minute). In 1952, Inge Edler and Helmuth Hertz recorded echoes from the heart and introduced this noninvasive method to look at the heart and great vessels.

Wars are bad, but they have led to many medical discoveries. It was found in World War II that the chest could be opened, and the damaged heart could be repaired. This opened the door for open-heart surgery. High-frequency sound could be thrown through the ocean, and if a submarine was present, its echo could be recorded. Now, we transmit high-frequency sounds across the chest of a patient, and the returning echoes outline the heart (Echocardiogram) This has improved so much that the heart can be imaged clearly, and its function can be determined. At about this time, Goffman introduced the ultracentrifuge for characterizing lipid abnormalities. In 1958 Mason Sones performed coronary arteriography, which has led to angioplasty, stents, and coronary bypass surgery. Treadmill exercise, ECG, vectorcardiography, imaging intensifier, right heart catheterization, angiography, and M-mode echo were further advanced. Holter monitoring, Judkins percutaneous catheterization, Swan Ganz catheter for measuring heart pressures, and 2-D echo became popular between 1960 and 1970. In 1970-1980, electrocardiographic interpretations were computerized. During this era, radionuclides, electrophysiological studies of the heart, and echo Doppler (records the movement of blood in the cardiovascular system) expanded the diagnostic procedures. Color Doppler, transesophageal echo, exercise echo, computed tomography (CT) and magnetic resonance imaging (MRI) of the heart were developed between 1980 and 1990. Since 1990 to the present time, radionuclide stress tests, event recorders for long-term detection of arrhythmias of the hearts, and electrophysiological studies were performed. Coronary calcium scores could be obtained from electron beam computed tomography and from CT of the heart. The laboratory test, C-reactive protein, (CRP), was performed to detect myocardial injury and inflammation. The brain natriuretic peptide (BNP) test indicated myocardial dysfunction. Lipid analysis was done by nuclear magnetic resonance (NMR) and electrophoresis.

All of these studies led to many therapeutic discoveries between 1940 and 1960 as nitrates, penicillin, mercurial diuretics, mitral- and aortic-valve surgery, and antiarrhythmic drugs. Better antiarrhythmic drugs, pacemakers with epicardial and transvenous leads, cardiopulmonary bypass, DC shock, and cardiopulmonary resuscitation (CPR) were advanced from 1950 to 1960. From 1960-1970 we saw many important discoveries such as the coronary care unit, lipid lowering drugs as the statins, coronary bypass surgery, intra-aortic balloon pump, and heart transplantation. Better diuretics like

Lasix, beta-blockers, and percutaneous coronary angioplasty were noted from 1970 to 1980. Calcium blockers, ACE inhibitors, thrombolytic agents, artificial hearts, advanced pacemakers, and internal cardiac defibrillators became available from 1980 to 1990. From 1990 to the present, new antihypertensive agents, new antiarrhythmic drugs, off-pump surgery, heart-failure drugs, radiofrequency ablation of arrhythmias, stents for coronary occlusion, heart transplants, and mechanical hearts were also being developed.

These are just a few of the many diagnostic and therapeutic advances that I have observed since 1950. I am certain in the future we will have many more. These have all come about because of the combination of physicians, researchers, and engineers working together. However, the cost has been tremendous.

A young man heard a lady screaming so he went into her home where she said that her baby could not breathe after swallowing a silver dollar. He immediately delivered a combination of back blows and chest thrusts until the silver dollar was expelled. The Heimlich thrust he knew was not recommended for infants since the abdominal thrust may damage the unprotected liver. The mother was so impressed she said, "You must be a doctor." He said, "No, I am a treasurer in our church."

Private insurance, Medicare, and Medicaid did not anticipate such major cost increases. Medicare is an entitlement program funded entirely at the federal level and focused primarily on people sixty-five-years or older (under sixty-five with certain disabilities). Medicaid is a combined federal and state program designed to pay medical costs for those with a limited income and resources. As health care costs soared, employers cut back benefits, insurance companies added exclusions, and many in the middle class found they had insecure protection. Many states used managed care (HMOs) to provide coverage for a significant proportion of Medicare enrollees. Often under the rubric of HMOs, independent practice associations (IPAs) and preferred provider insurance (PPI) have also developed. Some programs allow Medicaid recipients to have private insurance paid by Medicaid when it is found to be cost effective. This program is known as the health insurance premium payment program (HIPP). Consumers may choose a plan through a regional health-purchasing corporation (HIPC) instead of acquiring health coverage through employers. The HIPC, a public authority set up under a state commission would contract with various HMOs and other managed care plans as well as one plan offering free choice of providers. A payroll tax would allow revenue to flow into the HIPC to cover all state's citizens, except those eligible for federal programs. A universal insurance system that provides for consumer's choice among competing health plans has been suggested. Also, Medicare reimbursement has used a bundle payment. This is based on predetermined reimbursement rates for hospitals and physicians according to the patient's condition as classified in the diagnostic-related group (DRGs). This can be extended to outpatient care, home care, and nursing home care. Global budgeting (a negotiated cap on total expenditures) has also been suggested. The revenues from this would flow into the HIPC.

Primary care is attracting few new doctors because of paperwork, the demands of chronically sick, the need to bring work home, and many other factors. They do not want to fight the insurance companies. The salary gap is another major factor. Medicare's fee schedule pays less for office visits than simple procedures. No one is satisfied with the current formula by which Medicare calculates physician's fees. Medicare's projected spending growth is unsustainable. Medicare spending as a percentage of the gross domestic product is expected to nearly double in the next twenty years. Spending varies in various regions. There are variations in spending for physician services and there are also variations for fee for services. Both Medicare and Medicaid have cost containment problems.

A couple had financial problems and to increase their income decided that the wife should prostitute herself once a week. The first time, the husband waited until she came home at midnight. She said, "I made $125.25." He said, "You mean that one of those guys gave you only twenty-five cents?" She said, "No, they all did."

There are over 46 million uninsured people who don't qualify for entitlement programs. I am against universal or socialized medicine, and I am sure many average Americans would not willingly endorse such a program. However, to a degree we already have some elements of socialized medicine in Medicare and Medicaid. The rising cost of health care has been attributed to new technologies, malpractice litigation, the practice of defensive medicine, and an aging population. To solve the problem of cost is very complex, and many diverse solutions have been considered without success. I do think that in cardiology there is much room for a reduction of medical costs and related insurance premiums. Technology is advancing so rapidly that today's equipment may be obsolete tomorrow. We are now viewing the heart by computed tomography (CT) scans of the heart.

A man took his sick poodle to see a veterinarian. The vet said, "Your dog is dead." The man could not believe this. So the doctor had a Labrador retriever (Lab) go around the table and nothing happened. Still the man was not convinced, so the vet had a cat walk around the table and again nothing happened.

This convinced the man his poodle was dead. He asked, "How much do I owe you?" The doctor said, "One hundred and fifty dollars." The man asked, "Why so expensive?" The doctor said, "Fifty dollars for the lab tests and one hundred dollars for the CAT scan."

Advances in such imaging are not without a price. The computed tomography of the heart started with four-slice (detector) scanner. This has advanced to eight, sixteen, thirty-two, forty, sixty-four, dual source sixty-four (128) and soon 256 slices will be available. These advances each cost over two to three million dollars. This price can be reduced if hospitals begin to share such equipment. For example, should every hospital have a heart catheterization laboratory? University hospitals and regional hospitals can do more procedures than they are currently performing. Adding more procedures will reduce the cost since the overhead remains the same regardless of the number. The government needs to step in and control the number of catheterization labs. In addition, medical schools need to teach students the significance of a history and physical examination, as they did years ago. This can reduce the cost by decreasing the need for many tests. Often the tests are repeated without any definite indication such as a change in the person's symptoms or physical examination. In addition, controlling pharmaceutical advertisements, especially those on television, can reduce costs. I am sure that these advertisements do not influence many physicians. Patients need to know more about their medications, and this information is available from physicians and pharmacists. Expensive brochures describing drugs are sent to physicians, most of who throw them in the trashcan. Representative agents hired by pharmaceutical companies to promote their drugs can give this information to the physician at their office or in hospitals. Combining various drugs—polypill—is being investigated. Since many patients take two or more medications for illnesses, perhaps combining them would encourage compliance and reduce the cost. The greatest problem would be a drug reaction. Then each medication will have to be given separately to determine which caused the reaction. Since pharmaceutical companies have to experiment with many drugs and many are not successful, the government should help support some of these trials.

Because of better treatment and prevention of cardiovascular disease, we now have an aging population with conditions such as heart failure and Alzheimer's disease. We have shifted higher costs to the elderly. Seventy percent of the health care costs are generated by 10 percent of patients who have one or more chronic diseases. A high percentage of medical costs go to the care of the elderly in the last several months before death. If a patient is brain dead, why should he remain on a respirator and live for a few months longer at such great expense and grief to the family? The government needs to control this. This requires a cultural change within medicine and society. It remains uncertain whether online electronic medical records by physicians and hospitals will improve health care and decrease costs. Another aim to reduce Medicare spending is the concept of the *medical home* that the federal government is preparing to test. The core features include a physician-directed medical practice, a personal doctor for every patient, the capacity to coordinate high quality, accessible care, and payments that recognize a medical home added value for patients. It's hoped that it can produce long-term savings by reducing the number of avoidable emergency room visits and hospitalization for patients with serious chronic illness.

Doctors have increased their fees because of inflation and many are retiring early because of the great overhead expense of keeping an office and paying for malpractice insurance. Doctors are practicing defensive medicine for fear of malpractice lawsuits. I remember years ago I saw many patients in the emergency room with chest pain. If the pain was clearly musculoskeletal I did not order any studies but gave them medication for symptomatic relief. Today's doctors would order an ECG, chest X-ray, enzymes, CT scan of the heart or a nuclear stress test at a great cost to the person and to the insurance company. Tort reform is necessary but this has to be enacted by the government. With a decrease in overhead, doctors could lower their fees. Under these reductions, Medicare, Medicaid and private insurance premiums would stabilize.

Forty-six million people do not have health insurance because they do not qualify for Medicare or Medicaid and find private insurance too expensive. Very often this is the middle class and not the poor or the wealthy. The American Medical Association (AMA) suggested a plan for this. The AMA reform proposal has three pillars: 1) helping people buy health insurance through tax credits or vouchers; 2) providing a choice in health plans for individuals and families; 3) regulating the market and protecting high-risk patients. The government already gives financial assistance to buy private health insurance (over $125 billion per year). This supports an employee income tax break on job-based insurance. This gives more assistance to those in higher income brackets. Shifting some of the assistance to tax credits for lower-income people would reduce the number of uninsured. Tax credits are subtracted directly from an individual tax bill after calculations for tax brackets are made. Individuals with incomes too low to pay income tax still would be eligible for tax credits to buy health insurance. The dollar amount of tax credit should be inversely related to income. It is interesting that with this plan the government plays an important part. I remember years ago when doctors did not want Medicare. Memories can be very short.

A man asked another man if he was in New York on May 10, 2000. Since the second man had a poor memory, he opened his black book and turned to P for places. "Yes, I was in New York on May 10, 2000." The first man asked, "Did you meet a lady named Mary?" The other man said, "That would be under N for names. Yes, I met a lady called Mary." The first man said, "Did you take her to a bar for a drink?" The second man said, "That's under B. Yes, I took her to a bar." The first man said, "Next, did you go to a hotel?" The second man said, "That's under H. Yes I took her to a hotel." The first man said, "Did you make love to her?" The second man said, "That would be under L. Yes, I made love to her." The first man said, "I want you to know she's my wife, and I don't like it." The second man said, "Well, that's under O for opinion. I didn't like it either."

My late brother, Jimmy, and I often talked about health care and the economy. In fact, he describes his thoughts clearly in his book *Follow the Dollar*. Jimmy was a genius and a comedian. He thought he would live forever. He died at age ninety and on his deathbed he said to me, "Pete, I don't understand why the good Lord wants to take me in my prime." Our thinking is along these lines. Perhaps hospitals can be involved in insuring the 46 million uninsured and others. They already are involved with many insurance forms in an attempt to collect from insurance companies. There would be very little added expense to handle their own insurance coverage. The cost of health premiums should drop when the large insurance companies with their many employees and their highly paid CEOs face competition. Anyone who buys a policy from a hospital should have the liberty to select the hospital and doctor of his choice. Malpractice insurance would also be available in a hospital insurance plan for doctors. The government should back and insure each hospital's operation, so that the general public would feel secure in participating. The government should also subsidize the health care of indigents. Indigents are considered those who do not qualify for Medicaid and cannot afford private insurance. Many of these individuals are not aware of Medicaid and have not applied. In addition, many are reluctant to reveal their income. Others have transferred all their holdings to their children so that they may be declared indigent.

Each hospital should have a governing body of doctors, active and retired businessmen, and medical administrators to oversee the operation and enforce the rules and laws.

Politicians at present vary on their response to health care. Republicans would prefer to take tax health benefits from the workplace and give families tax credits, relying on free market competition. Democrats would depend more on government. The mandate is that every American has some type of health coverage. There are too many uninsured.

Three men on a beach saw a person with long hair and a white robe come out of the ocean. He said to the first man, "Do you know who I am?" The man said, "Yes, you are Jesus Christ." Jesus said, "Do you have any problems?" He said, "Yes, I was in World War II and was shot in the shoulder. I have not been able to use my shoulder since." Jesus touched him and said, "Have faith, and you will be able to use your shoulder." He asked the second man, "Do you know who I am?" He said, "Yes, you are Jesus." Jesus said, "Anything wrong with you?" He stated, "I was in the Vietnam War and was shot in the hip. Now I cannot walk well." Jesus asked him to pray and touched him, and he was able to walk. He looked at the third man. He said, "Do you know who I am?" The third man said, "Yes, but don't touch me, I am on total disability."

A most effective way to reduce disease and improve the quality of life is through preventive care. Frequent checkups, exercise, not smoking, control of hypertension, and treatment of diabetes and abnormal lipids should be encouraged. Medical schools need to emphasize preventative medicine. More people die of neglect each year than are killed in our wars. We want cost control, but we also should have broad access to health care, quality control, and continued advances in medical science. The vast majority say that health care should be reformed with respect to access, quality, and cost. This can be accomplished by the cooperation of physicians, American Medical Association, American Hospital Association, pharmaceutical associations, Advanced Medical Technology Association, the private sector, government, and others. Medicine is at a crossroads, but all problems should be solved for the good of the patient. Health care is on everyone's mind. This should not discourage young individuals from seeking a career in medicine. I hope young people will read my autobiography and realize that they can overcome obstacles.

A story is told about an ant. It was dragging a piece of straw that was very large for him, and he stood out among the other ants. He was moving well when he had to cross a break in the ground. He pondered as to how he would go across and pull the straw. He placed the straw across the break, and he walked on the straw to the other side. On the other side he pulled the straw across. This is an example of one way to overcome an obstacle. People have many obstacles during their life. They must face them calmly. Don't rush. Wait, and often you will have a better insight into the problem.

Be determined, persistent, and motivated, and you will overcome any obstacles—just as the ant and I did *through the back door.*

9915618R0

Made in the USA
Lexington, KY
08 June 2011